CHARLES-FERDINAND RAMUZ

Jean-Luc Persecuted

TRANSLATED FROM THE FRENCH BY
OLIVIA BAES

DEEP VELLUM PUBLISHING

DALLAS, TEXAS

Deep Vellum Publishing
3000 Commerce St., Dallas, Texas 75226
deepvellum.org · @deepvellum

Deep Vellum is a 501c3 nonprofit literary arts organization
founded in 2013 with the mission to bring
the world into conversation through literature.

Originally published in the French language in 1908 by Librairie académique *Didier, Perrin et Cie* in Paris, France. This translation based on the 1995 Les Cahiers Rouges edition published by Grasset in Paris.
English translation copyright © 2020 by Olivia Baes
First edition, 2020
All rights reserved.

Support for this publication has been provided in part by grants from the National Endowment for the Arts, the Texas Commission on the Arts, the City of Dallas Office of Arts and Culture's ArtsActivate program, and the Moody Fund for the Arts:

This publication has been made possible with financial support from the Swiss Arts Council Pro Helvetia

swiss arts council
pr⊃helvetia

ISBNs: 978-1-64605-016-1 (paperback) | 978-1-64605-017-8 (ebook)

LIBRARY OF CONGRESS CATALOGING IN PUBLICATION DATA
Names: Ramuz, C. F. (Charles Ferdinand), 1878-1947, author. | Baes, Olivia, translator.
Title: Jean-Luc persecuted / Charles-Ferdinand Ramuz ; translated from the French by Olivia Baes.
Other titles: Jean-Luc persécuté. English
Description: First edition. | Dallas, Texas : Deep Vellum Publishing, 2020.
  | Originally published in the French language in 1908 by Librairie académique Didier, Perrin et Cie in Paris, France. This translation based on the 1995 Les Cahiers Rouges edition published by Grasset in Paris.
Identifiers: LCCN 2020018713 (print) | LCCN 2020018714 (ebook) | ISBN 9781646050161 (paperback) | ISBN 9781646050178 (ebook)
Classification: LCC PQ2635.A35 J413 2020   (print) | LCC PQ2635.A35 (ebook)
  | DDC 843/.914--dc23
LC record available at https://lccn.loc.gov/2020018713
LC ebook record available at https://lccn.loc.gov/2020018714

Cover art by Chad Felix | chadfelix.com
Interior layout and typesetting by Kirby Gann
Text set in Bembo, a typeface modeled on typefaces cut by Francesco Griffo for Aldo Manuzio's printing of *De Aetna* in 1495 in Venice.

PRINTED IN THE UNITED STATES OF AMERICA

"Ramuz wrote, many years ago, some thirty works, of which *Jean-Luc* [*Persecuted*] is perhaps one of the best . . . a writer who breaks all molds." —Juan Rulfo

═══════════════

The wind had picked up again, warmer, the wind called the snow-eater; the dark layers widened; the pond blackened, cracked: one day the water was liberated. And so the dead frogs floated back up from the bottom, and the murders of crows flew in circles around them. The shadows arrived; there was the forest's darkness, a blue-black on the mountain, a sky that remained burdened, and some scattered islands of light. Again, she called him. But he answered her: "Never."

═══════════════

"With the grim logic of a classical tragedy, terrible things begin to happen . . . a painful tale of isolation and woe that resembles nothing so much as *Frankenstein* save that Mary Shelley's monster had a richer vocabulary. Plainly, even matter-of-factly written, the story is a downer but an affecting one that leaves readers wishing that Jean-Luc had had better luck." —*Kirkus Reviews*

CONTENTS

Vaud Damned:
A Note on the Translation

One man's madness in the face of Vaud, its valleys, its ridges, its snow—piling up only to melt, be forgotten, with the many flowers that rise every Easter, then collapse and rise once again—with the village that stirs, and the echoes of women, their laughter, and the men with their axes and carts, calls for a special kind of momentum—one that Franco-Swiss writer Charles-Ferdinand Ramuz obsessively referred to as his *élan* in his journal. This momentum, as he wrote in an entry dated May 1909, came and went as it pleased, "simply carried him."[1]

For me, Ramuz's momentum always summons the wind. It was the natural force that propelled his inspiration and the way he used language, a force hailing directly from a Swiss region called the Canton of Vaud. And though his language was technically French, from a very young age, Ramuz knew this French to be quite different from the language in his school books. His was a French

---

1. C.F. Ramuz, "Journal, notes et brouillons," *Tome* 2, 1904–1920, Slatkine, entry dated May 10, 1909.

he believed had not yet been written down, a language spurred on by his authentic experience of that small and secluded region he called home.[2]

In his famous 1924 letter to his editor Bernard Grasset, Ramuz—responding to claims by some of his contemporaries that he "wrote badly on purpose"—expanded on his relationship to French. To him, "correct" French—or "classic" French, as he dubbed it himself—was nothing but an academic language sequestered from experience, one that he did not feel was valid for him, who had grown up in another country, one that was divided from France by a literal border. But what upset him most in that statement was the popular belief that he wrote badly "on purpose":

> Need I tell you that this accusation is by far the most serious of all for me, the only one that actually affects me? It runs precisely in the opposite direction to all my tendencies, to all my research; it affects me right at the center, —as on the contrary I have always tried to be truthful and "wrote badly" precisely only out of a need

---

2. "O accent, you are in our words, and you are the indication, but you are not yet in our written language. You are in the gesture, you are in the allure, all the way to the very languid step of the one who comes back from mowing down his meadow or trimming his vineyard: consider this gait and the fact that our phrases don't have it." *Raison d'être: Par C.F. Ramuz*, 1914, Lausanne C. Tarin, Cahier Vaudois 1, ebook, https://archive.org/details/raisondtreparc00ramuuoft/page/n10 (English translation by Olivia Baes and Emma Ramadan).

to be more truthful or, if you will, more authentic, to be as true, as authentic as possible.[3]

This was not the first time Ramuz sought to defend what many considered to be his incorrect use of French. In 1914, back in Switzerland after more than a decade in Paris, he wrote a manifesto entitled *Raison d'être*, in which he explored his Vaudois roots and what they had come to mean to him as a writer. In the text, he revealed the uncomfortable feeling he had of living in France's capital. There, he felt totally out of place, which, ironically, was emphasized by the fact that, unlike the British or Spanish tourists, he spoke the language—but very differently than the French themselves. His rhythm, so out of step with theirs, embarrassed him at every turn, shining a bright light on his difference. In *Raison d'être*, Ramuz contrasts the two languages at length:

Of what use are these "qualities" to me given

---

3. "Ai-je besoin de vous dire que cette accusation est de beaucoup pour moi la plus grave de toutes, la seule à vrai dire qui me touche? Elle va très exactement en sens inverse de toutes mes tendances, de toutes mes recherches; elle me touche au point central, – ayant toujours tâché au contraire d'être véridique et ne m'étant mis à « mal écrire » que précisément par souci d'être plus vrai ou, si on veut, plus authentique, d'être aussi vrai, d'être aussi authentique que possible." Lettre à Bernard Grasset, page 14, https://ebooks-bnr.com/ebooks/pdf4/ramuz_lettre_a_bernard_grasset.pdf, bibliothèque numérique romande d'après C. F. Ramuz, Œuvres complètes 11, Lettre à Grasset, Salutation paysanne, Passage du Poète, Autre lettre, Cézanne, Lausanne, H. L. Mermod, s.d. [1941].

as such in manuals estranged from the object—
for example a certain elegance (for I care deeply
about the other), lightness, speed—if the line of
a hill before me takes so long to reach its summit, if such a mass of abrupt faces holds beauty
only in its heaviness, if the labored appearance of
a gesture, the furrowing of a forehead on which
expression takes shape only little by little, oppose
themselves to this boasted elegance? What does
ease matter to me if I have to render clumsiness,
what does a fixed order matter to me if I want
to give the impression of disorder, what to do
with the much-too-airy when I'm in the presence of the compact and cluttered? We need to
have made our rhetoric on the spot, down to
our grammar, our syntax.[4]

In 1907, Ramuz was commissioned to write *Le petit village dans la montagne* by Lausanne editor Edouard Payot.
Acutely aware of his linguistic difference, he left Paris in
order to live between the two small Franco-Swiss villages
of Chandolin and Lens. The book's purpose was to docu-
ment the village and its customs, legends, inhabitants, and
natural surroundings. Like a fly on the wall, for months, the
somewhat timid Ramuz recorded everything he saw and
heard in these villages. It is no wonder then that *Jean-Luc*

---

4. *Raison d'être: Par C.F. Ramuz*, 1914, Lausanne C. Tarin, Cahier
Vaudois 1, ebook, https://archive.org/details/raisondtreparc00
ramuuoft/page/n10 (English translation by Olivia Baes and Emma
Ramadan).

persécuté directly followed *Le petit village dans la montagne*; its intention feels remarkably similar: to somehow capture a place's rhythm—that organic connection between the villagers and their surroundings—in writing. On April 5, 1908, while writing *Jean-Luc persécuté*, Ramuz had a break-through entry: "My style must have the gait of my characters."[5] *Démarche*, the French word for *gait*, can also mean *approach* and *process*. This novel would become a prime example of his very important artistic realization.

Translating *Jean-Luc persécuté*, one must keep Ramuz's firm stance of authenticity in mind. The author did not mean for his French to sound "correct." Just as *Jean-Luc persécuté* did not read as fluent to the average French reader in 1908, *Jean-Luc Persecuted* is not meant to enter English fluidly over a century later. As Ramuz put it himself, again in his letter to Grasset: "The man who truly expresses himself does not translate. He allows the movement to form within him until its completion, allowing this same movement to group words in its own way."[6] Ramuz's idiosyncratic and varying punctuation moves us through Jean-Luc's journey with emotion as catalyst. Sentences organize themselves according to sight and feeling.

---

5. C.F. Ramuz, "Journal, notes et brouillons," *Tome* 2, 1904–1920, Slatkine, entry dated April 5, 1908.

6. "L'homme qui s'exprime vraiment ne traduit pas. Il laisse le mouvement se faire en lui jusqu'à son terme, laissant ce même mouvement grouper les mots à sa façon." Lettre à Bernard Grasset, 14, https://ebooks-bnr.com/ebooks/pdf4/ramuz_lettre_a_bernard_grasset.pdf, Bibliothèque numérique romande d'après C. F. Ramuz,

Perhaps this is why Ramuz thought his writing—
one he insisted was grounded in what he called "gesture-language"—was closest to cinema.[7] As his translator,
I chose to follow this cinematic momentum, picking
rhythm and emotion over the grammatical and syntacti-
cal rules we are told are "correct" and cannot be broken.
In the novel, which itself begins in movement, Jean-Luc's
rhythm moves us immediately. As he returns home to
find his wife Christine missing, we are sent on an anx-
ious walk to retrieve her, following her footsteps in the
snow through the woods, the trail, and the mountains,
where fleeting observations of nature intermingle with
Jean-Luc's own anguished guesses about where his wife
might be:

> He had set off again, he began to walk faster, he
> quickly arrived at the crest; there, you enter a
> comb, the trail goes off down the middle. Larches
> the color of honey, their trunks gray, gray in
> certain branches already skinned, looked to be
> arranged all around; up ahead, from a gash in

Œuvres complètes 11, Lettre à Grasset, Salutation paysanne, Passage du
Poète, Autre lettre, Cézanne, Lausanne, H. L. Mermod, s.d. [1941].

7. "I also see that this gesture-language (which is another encouragement), that this language-following-gestures, where logic gives
way to the very rhythm of the images, is not far from what cinema is attempting to accomplish through its own means." "*Je vois
aussi que cette langue-geste (c'est un autre encouragement), que cette langue-
suite-de-gestes, où la logique cède le pas au rythme même des images, n'est
pas très loin de ce que cherche à réaliser avec ses moyens à lui le cinéma.*"
Lettre à Bernard Grasset, 27, https://ebooks-bnr.com/ebooks/

the green sky, a faraway summit appeared, pink.
There was a little pink too, almost blond rather,
in the light, on the snow, while various dips and
ridges, in this velvet, sparkled like gold, like so on
a bush, the tip of a tree, a rift in the terrain.

The opening paragraphs of the book allow us into the
real-time collision of Jean-Luc's inner and outer worlds.
Grammatically speaking, more semicolons should figure
throughout, but I chose to forgo them all, as the com-
mas are a perfect reminder that we are on the move with
Jean-Luc, right there along with him, seeing the crest, the
comb, and the trail the moment they pop up.

It was with this same emotive rhythm in mind that
I chose to keep the novel's frequent use of repetition. In
most cases, what could be regarded as bad and awkward
writing is telling, which is the case when Christine, who
has just admitted her affair to Jean-Luc, hovers near the
front stoop, waiting to see what her crestfallen husband
will do next:

Meanwhile there was movement in the kitchen,
the footsteps moved away, a door creaked, the
footsteps were in the bedroom, the footsteps
returned. Suddenly they came closer, she turned

pdf4/ramuz_lettre_a_bernard_grasset.pdf, bibliothèque numérique
romande d'après C. F. Ramuz, *Œuvres complètes* 11, Lettre à Grasset,
Salutation paysanne, Passage du Poète, Autre lettre, Cézanne, Lausanne,
H. L. Mermod, s.d. [1941].

around; at that very moment he passed by her. He had on his hat, the child on one arm, under the other a bag; he walked down the stairs. She said: "What are you doing?" She repeated: "Jean-Luc what are you doing?" but it was too late. He was already off in the distance. He walked toward the village.

Here, the tension between Christine's rising anxiety and Jean-Luc's cold resolve defines this crucial narrative moment in which he decides to leave her. Ramuz's use of calm repetition mimics Jean-Luc's determined footsteps as he goes, the incredulous Christine looking on, somewhat hoping he will turn back, herself caught between the repetition of her own question, one she seems to be asking to convince herself he is not really leaving. In translation, the tempo of this moment, which is established by the use of repetition and the emotive order of the action, is crucial, and I felt it was important to keep it as is.

The novel is equally brilliant in its navigation of Jean-Luc's tumultuous and changing emotional terrain and the village's own contrasting seasons: from the slow and harsh winter—with its thudded footsteps, whispers behind the inn's door, and long stares into the cracks of the wooden ceiling—to its more chipper summer—with its lovers in meadows, idle gossip under the linden tree, and drunken chatter in the cellar. Guiding us through both these landscapes is the French pronoun *on*.

An all-seeing pronoun that allows us to experience Jean-Luc's journey from every eye and ear in the village, only increasing our protagonist's paranoia, while also heightening the overall claustrophobic feel of the story, which, nestled in between the village and its high mountains, seems only to lead to one thing: Jean-Luc's demise.

On is always difficult to translate in English, but here, in order to maintain its full effect and really draw the reader into the story, I often opted for "you," which, as it accrues, seems to carry us through Jean-Luc's misadventures, placing us directly in his wake. A good example of this also hails from the first walk we take alongside Jean-Luc as he searches for the missing Christine:

> But the heart is sad, and all was in silence. A chough in flight passed now and again in the sky, where it occupied a space, then no longer occupied it; sounds came from very far off, like strangers to the land: you heard the village bell ring, you didn't know from where, maybe in the prairie, soon it hushed; a gunshot blasted, a poacher's, in a gorge all the way over there, which dragged out for a long time, jarred into echoes.

Here, we hear the village bell ring, we don't know from where, soon it stops ringing. A gunshot blasts, and we hear that, too, in a gorge, all the way over there. We hear it drag on for a time. I thought it was important to have the reader become a part of the story so that when the heart is sad, just before, ours is too, in the silence set to reveal that Christine, Jean-Luc's wife, is laughing somewhere in a wood with her lover, Augustin. Something about using the "you" just felt right for this story—perhaps even its cinematic feel as it guides us along, allowing us to empathize further with a man whose destiny, like an avalanche, begins to tumble toward us the moment we start reading.

Though Ramuz wrote in a French that stemmed from a specific part of the world, his stories are universal in the human suffering they explore. *Jean-Luc persécuté* is a prime example. It may recount the story of a peasant very much born and raised in the Canton of Vaud, but Jean-Luc's despair—linked as it may be to the foreign land he moves through—is recognizably human. Even if his tale is extraordinary—with entire chapters in which he believes his child to be alive though he has recently drowned—the emotions that catalyze his unusual madness are ones we can most likely all relate to on some level. In order for us to empathize with Jean-Luc and experience the total misery that is his life, Ramuz takes us down a literal and linguistic path we may not be accustomed to or comfortable with, but one that will jar us into echoes of feeling.

As I translated *Jean-Luc persécuté*, I chose to stay true to Ramuz's artistic purpose, refusing to tame my own writing for a more fluid reading experience in English, which I believed would greatly harm the story and the particular suspense that arises from its singular rhythm. In another one of his 1908 journal entries, Ramuz calls the effect of this rhythm, the "tone," "a way of seeing and feeling things that, once achieved, becomes the tone and to which everything must be sacrificed." As Ramuz's translator, I also chose to sacrifice everything to this unique way of seeing and feeling things, and only in doing so was able to arrive at Jean-Luc's persecution—his own sacrifice—which though universal in resonance, begins as an echo in the Canton of Vaud, and should remain there, resounding from there, in all of its translations, whatever their language may be.

Olivia Baes
September 2019
Cabanelles, Catalunya, Spain

Jean-Luc Persecuted

to

Albert Muret

who's from up there

CHAPTER I

SEEING AS IT HAD BEEN AGREED he would go, that
Sunday, to see a goat in Sasseneire, Jean-Luc Robille, after
eating, grabbed hold of his hat and baton. He then went
to kiss his wife (for he liked her and they'd only been
married two years). She asked him:

—When will you be back?

He answered:

—Around six o'clock.

He continued:

—I've got to hurry because Simon's waiting for me,
and he doesn't like to be kept waiting.

However, before leaving the house, walking on tiptoe, he went into the bedroom and up to the cradle
where the little one, whom they'd had together the year
before, slept. "Be careful!" cried Christine. And he, bending over, did not kiss him as he'd intended to, but only
watched him sleep. He was a big boy, eleven months and
two weeks old (for you count the weeks and days in the
start), with cheeks that looked varnished, and a big round
head, deep in the crease of the pillow. The cradle had been

made with beautiful larch by Jean-Luc himself, who had done carpenter's work (as they say) and learned the ropes, before taking on his mother's property, when his father was still alive. So he remained perched there a moment, watching the little one sleep. Then, he crossed the kitchen once more and opened the door: "Adieu, wife!" he said again, and again he kissed Christine.

He found Simon in bed.

—Listen, said Simon, my pains have gotten hold of me again; so, never mind today!

—We'll go next Sunday, said Jean-Luc.

He had taken a seat near the bed; he chatted with Simon for some time, and with his daughter who had come; the three of them chatted as to pass the time; one o'clock sounded, then two o'clock. Upon which, Jean-Luc headed back. At the inn, he came across a crowd, which made him lose another fifteen minutes. However, when he was invited to come in for a drink, he refused. And the others began to laugh: "Are you still drinking? Is it allowed or not?" "Oh! it's allowed!" said Jean-Luc. He laughed too, then quickly went home.

He went up the stairs, pushed against the latch, the door was locked. He thought: "She went to Marie's" (Marie was the blacksmith's wife), and, bending down, took the key from under the woodpile where they hid it. Then thought: "I'll go have a look at Marie's." He didn't find her there, and Marie hadn't seen Christine, nor Marie's husband, who was reading the newspaper, who looked up and said to Jean-Luc, because he liked to tease: "Wives should never be left on their own." Jean-Luc didn't answer, he was worried.

Worry had come to him all of a sudden, he did not know why, and it followed him into the empty kitchen, to the dying fire, and into the bedroom, where he sat near the cradle and listened to Sunday. The sound of voices, and a trickle of water, nothing more; everyone rested.

It had snowed a little the night before, a trifle again, a sprinkle, only marking that winter was there, and in the morning broad daylight had entered the bedroom, where all seemed wholly restored. He sat with his elbows on his knees, he asked himself: "Where could she have gone?" He didn't have the answer.

And so, seized by boredom, he stood up, he looked out the window. There was the tip of the meadow's slope, then came willows and aspens, and the large pond appeared, round and not yet frozen; but, usually beautiful as it glistened and reflected the whole of the mountain, the snow had melted on the pond and seemed to have tarnished it. In the back, beneath the blue sky, the mountain zones ascended, all white, stained with black.

Suddenly, Jean-Luc's eyes reached the ground and lingered there. It was because of the footprints. Footprints in the snow, small, pronounced. And they didn't head toward the village, where the path was already open, but to the other side, by the pond. He thought: "Where did she go?"

7

In a flash, he was decided. He took the little one who woke, wrapped him in a warm shawl, then, returning to Marie's: "Will you look after him while I'm gone?" Marie asked: "Christine hasn't come home?" He said no, returned to the house, but didn't enter it; he began to follow the tracks. They started right in front of the door; he followed them without seeming to, his hands in his pockets, because of the people who could see him, but his heart beat hard in his chest; and he hoped again that once on the path that followed the bank at the back of the pond, the footprints would turn toward the village; no, not at all: they did turn, but in the other direction, in the direction of the mountain.

So he went off again more quickly. Now, on the path, the tracks were muddled, a mule and some men had also passed this way, but he watched the sides, where the layers of snow were still smooth; and, indeed, soon he saw the small footprints take a left toward some kind of fold in the terrain, like there are everywhere in the region, of which he followed the back, and was led directly to a slope where he began to climb.

On the well-exposed banks, the snow had already melted, allowing yellow layers of turf to pierce through; there, the traces suddenly ceased, but only to reappear higher up, and indeed, in the humid soil, the heel had sunk deeper, and the shoes' hobnails had scratched the surface by slipping, there was no room for error; now, crosswise, he went off toward another way that leads to Le

Plateau des Roffes. He thought: "She made a detour!" He thought, looking at the hobnails' marks: "And she kept her Sunday shoes on." He clearly recognized the hobnails' pattern, planted only around the sole and at the round and smooth tip, for these shoes were a present he had given her, when he had returned from the autumn fair. Then he thought: "What small feet she has!" While a voice inside of him repeated: "Dear small feet, dear small feet, the prettiest there are!"

Nevertheless he continued, and he reached the second path. This path is rocky in the summer, lit up with sun, pretty wild rose bushes bearing small leaves and pink flowers; the snow had covered everything up, the bushes looked like big balls of unraveled yarn. Then, as you reach higher up, when you turn around, you glimpse straight beneath you all of the village houses, pressed together and tucked away in the crater like eggs in a nest, roofs white among the white, and the tall church in the middle with its bare walls; then from behind, carved out against the sky and the depth of the large valley, a strange sharp hill rises up, with edges like a saw's teeth because of its fir trees, Le Bourni, as they call it.

That was the view, he went up. From among the bushes, at one point, comes a tall solitary pine. Arrived there, Jean-Luc abruptly halted. For he had just seen a second trace. This second trace joined the other one under the pine. They were big footprints, a man's footprints; and, under the pine, someone must have waited, the snow having been trodden upon; then the big footprints and the small footprints had continued on together, as could be seen farther down the trail of marks at times farther apart, at times closer together, sometimes nearly muddled.

He opened his eyes, he couldn't believe it and yet he was forced to, for the layer of snow became thicker, having been crammed into crevices by the wind; so, as far as you could see on this shoulder of the hill, indicated in blue by a shadow, the deep holes continued on like the seam to a sheet.

He had set off again, he began to walk faster, he quickly arrived at the crest; there, you enter a comb, the trail goes off down the middle. Larches the color of honey, their trunks gray, gray in certain branches already skinned, looked to be arranged all around; up ahead, from a gash in the green sky, a faraway summit appeared, pink. There was a little pink too, almost blonde rather, in the light, on the snow, while various dips and ridges, in this velvet, sparkled like gold, like so on a bush, the tip of a tree, a rift in the terrain.

But the heart is sad, and all was in silence. A chough in flight passed now and again in the sky, where it occupied a space, then no longer occupied it; sounds came from very far off, like strangers to the land: you heard the village bell ring, you didn't know from where, maybe in the prairie, soon it hushed; a gunshot blasted, a poacher's, in a gorge all the way over there, which dragged out for a long time, jarred into echoes.

And Jean-Luc brushed his hand against his forehead, for he was sweating, but he didn't halt: now he would have had his eyes closed, guessing it all. He went up the comb, took another right; then, among the first larches, headed toward the forest. He entered the forest. Suddenly there was another place that had been trampled upon; following which, he could only distinguish a single trace, that of the man's big footprints.

He examined it: no, only one, his legs failed him; he thought: "He had to have carried her; she was tired, he carried her!" And indeed the traces were deeper than before, more dragged, with here and there a stone popping up and under the trees a little black earth or the needles of larches; elsewhere someone had banged into a hidden root, then had rested; and that is when the two small feet appeared once more.

It was as he had predicted. At the edge of the forest, there was a new hayloft belonging to a man named Augustin Crettaz. "It's him!" thought Jean-Luc. "But they told me he was away, so it must be that he's back, and she didn't tell me!" He was leaning against a tree, he watched. You couldn't hear anything, you couldn't see anything, there must have been hay, it's comfortable to lie in hay. He moved as if to go forward, but at that moment someone, over there, began to laugh; he knew this laugh well; he hurried back down.

It was five o'clock when she returned, and the day was coming to a close (for it was during one of the shortest days of the year). At the same time, the cold of the winter nights lowered itself down, the cold that surprises flowing water and hardens paths. Then the bell-ringer came out of the inn, began to walk up the high stairs of the church tower, for the time of the angelus had come.

She was surprised to find the kitchen door not fully closed. She walked in; a little daylight still filtered through the window, she saw Jean-Luc sitting by the fireplace.

No fire, and the ash died-out; he sat there. She said to him:

—How come you're back already?

He answered:

—I never left, Simon was sick.

Her shoulders fidgeted, but at once the movement was contained, and he did not notice, leaning as he was; in fact he was not watching her, he stared at the floor before him.

She went on:

—Aren't you cold without the fire? It's starting to freeze.

Jean-Luc responded:

—I'm not cold.

The angelus rang, they both remained quiet. Jean-Luc kept his head lowered, the child was lying in his arms. He was starting to become heavy, for he was falling asleep: a child sleeps and eats like this all day long. The angelus came to an end, the little eyelids unfolded, and a more crimson blood spread under the skin, with the dampness of sleep.

—Has he eaten? said Christine.

Jean-Luc answered:

—That's my business.

She was starting the fire. At once, she was vivid with light. And so what had not been visible now showed. Her hair, a bit disheveled, fell on her forehead in small curls (that were usually so smooth), and drops glittered there, trapped; the fake gold needle she kept at the top of her camisole was fastened on crooked; on her shoulders, and her chest, were wet stains. Jean-Luc had turned toward her.

—I didn't think it was raining?

—Those are the drops falling from the rooftops.

She said this with confidence. And then abruptly, going to him:

—Give me the child a minute.

He shook his head.

She didn't insist, she didn't even seem surprised; and continued to tidy up, coming and going through the kitchen, taking the cups and dishes to the rack; the pot was on the fire, she went down to the cellar to cut a slab of cheese, she brought the bread; the water started to boil, she poured it into the coffee press. The noise of those little drops that pierce through the filter and fall into the tinplate recipient sounded; upon which, they dwindled, and the milk came to a boil:

—You can come now, she said, it's ready.

The child was completely asleep. Yet Jean-Luc had not left him; and, coming to sit at the table, did not leave him; he lifted him with precaution, and laid him down on his knees with one leg slightly raised. Christine no longer said anything.

They sat facing each other, the width of the table between them; there, the flat bread roll was set down, and the pot of milk and the cheese, which she cut with her knife and began to eat at once. She had also filled the ceramic cups with their yellow interior; the coffee was steaming with its good smell. She ate and drank. Jean-Luc had also cut from the bread roll, had started to eat, but the bites didn't go down, even though he usually had a big appetite, for he was a strong and good worker. But now the bread felt like dry earth in his mouth, so he drank to make it go down, but his plate remained full, while Christine had had another helping and filled her cup again. She asked him:

—What's wrong?

He pushed his plate away, let his knife fall onto the table, hung his head, and remained.

She went on:

—Jean-Luc!

He didn't move, he was absent; and his hands slipped off the side of the table, his big empty hands hung there.

She saw that they needed to talk.

—Listen, she said, we should hear each other out.

I'm sure you remember, the day of the Patron, when you asked me, when you said that you loved me, and I answered: "I like Augustin better, and he's asked me too, but his father is against it because I'm too poor, and I've had enough of being a servant in other people's homes, so let's get engaged if you'd like; but if Augustin wants to kiss me, I'll let myself be kissed." Is that not what I told you?

He didn't answer, she continued:

—And when your mother was against it too and you went to her and said: "I don't care what you think!" didn't I give you a piece of advice: "Listen," I said, "don't quarrel with her, it's bad luck. You'll find another." And you didn't listen to me. Is that not the truth, too?

She waited, nothing came; she went on:

—And since you kept coming to visit me and came around all the time, didn't I say: "You're not like the others." And I said: "On top of it, you're too thin." You laughed. Well, is that not true?

Again she stopped; it was no use.

—So what? he came back, he asked to see me, we went to fetch hay together. And if you snuck up from behind, what can I do about it?

Having spoken, she hushed; he was still quiet. There was a big log on the fireplace; eaten away in the middle, it suddenly broke in half, and one of the pieces rolled through the ash. Pointing at the child, Christine said again:

—Give him to me, you hear.

But he had moved back abruptly and, making a gesture with his hand as if to push her away from him:

—You will no longer touch him!

She shrugged her shoulders, she said: "I've got someone to comfort me."

She opened the door, she went out on the stoop and leaned against the railing.

There was no moon, but many stars, beautiful and white, as if made of glass, which seemed to hang from threads, moving together in the wind: they barely lit up anything. And beneath the great darkness of the sky and the shadows, the snow was strange to behold, with its vast white sweep, the gleam that came from it, and in the middle, the pond all dark, the snow having melted on it. Christine held her shawl tight.

Then, leaning away from the stoop, she looked toward the village, which you can barely see from behind the corner of the house; she looked at a certain window. The squares of the roofs were marked in white, and the walls of dark wood, as if come undone and dissolved in the night, appeared to be suspended in midair. There was this dot of light, like a red eye, that was all.

Meanwhile there was movement in the kitchen, the footsteps moved away, a door creaked, the footsteps were in the bedroom, the footsteps returned. Suddenly they came closer, she turned around; at that very moment he passed by her. He had on his hat, the child on one arm, under the other a bag; he walked down the stairs. She said: "What are you doing?" She repeated: "Jean-Luc what are you doing?" but it was too late. He was already off in the distance. He walked toward the village.

The next day, it was said he had gone down to his mother's, and it was confirmed when Félicie, the little servant, came on his behalf to get the two cows and the goat.

CHAPTER II

ON THIS SUNDAY IN MARCH, the carillon having rung around nine o'clock, the path that climbs from the bottom filled with people, for it was the season where nearly the entire village had moved down there.

They came from warmth, they headed for the cold, they found snow there.

There was still a rather thick layer of it, especially on this steep face of the mountain; it had barely melted around the tree trunks; in such a way that the trail, just wide enough for passage, was bordered by two little white walls.

Where people walked, ascending in a long line, men with their hands in their pockets, girls holding their shawls tight; and in the distance, through the slope, the sound of laughter and voices could be heard. Then suddenly, the slope breaks, and the entire village appears at once, raising its tall church in the air, at the bottom of which are houses tightly pressed together.

You're in the village the moment you see it, so to speak; first comes the mill with its very old wheel, at a halt, because of Sabbath, then comes the wheat shed and barns; finally the road veers a little, to arrive between two rows of small gardens with gray gates, and in the back, houses, nearly all of them shut on that day. Yet, at one of them, a door occasionally opened, and someone came out in their Sunday clothes, mixing together with those on the road.

And the closer you got, the louder the carillon grew, composed of six bells, all six in movement, swinging and spinning through the air with their heavy tempo, and at times delayed, or else hurried, colliding and dividing.

Little by little, it stopped; other ringing followed, the biggest of the bells rang on the fly; the sound of voices was drowned out, as well as the crackle of ice fragments under large heavy shoes; there were still more people, late, who hurried; following which, the bells rang for the start of mass. And in the village and the fields, everything was calm and deserted as far as the eye could see.

Alone, near the cemetery, in front of an old house, five or six men had remained chatting on a heap of beams. It was warm there, the sun having just come out from behind sluggish clouds; it gathered the courage to heat up the dark wood and the wall. They had lit their pipes, belonging to those who still come up for mass, but no longer attend to it, except on days of great celebration; and thus do without the Good Lord, only remembering him at the hour of death.

They chatted, then remained a long time without saying anything. At times an idea crosses your mind and you take the pipe out of your mouth to make it known; following which, you take up the pipe again, you wait for another to come, as they did, with the organ's stormy sound and the voices of cantors in the great silence. And they looked ahead of themselves, through the meadows that descended in soft beautiful folds, the small bare trees that seemed to be made of rusted iron, while a cloud hung over Le Bourni like a broken wing.

But the great wind of the organ picked up strongly once more, and, as if the clouds had obeyed it, at once the sun was covered again; the men buttoned up their jackets, or they beat their feet on the hardened earth; the organ died down once more: suddenly the hour of the Elevation rang; they took off their hats, all together they went to the church.

At the bottom of the big gray wall is a very small door, pierced and painted blue; there's nothing on it, no windows or ornaments, nothing but the door; it was closed, and right against it, ears pressed, two leaning men listened. Opposite was the cemetery, large and square between its low walls of rough stone, with its black metal gate that bears a skull and crossbones, and no trees inside, but the colored crosses with their tops shaped like triangles, and in the back another tall cross made of stone. And the snow covered everything, except that it was now slightly slumped around the edges of tombs, which appeared in single file, like little white beds. It made you think: "At least they're warm under there."

The organ's rumble now shook the walls, then the cantors' voices started again, then came silence once more; then, the door having opened, the crowd began to emerge. And the others, having approached, were leaning against the cemetery wall, and watched. They emerged silently; the crowd of people, at first pressed together in the narrow opening, went on to scatter outside with difficulty: very old women weighed down by age, knotted with large bones under the dresses that had become too big for them, and the old men too wore clothes too big, clothes that had been made for their wedding day, the girls pretty in their Sunday dress and lowering their heads beneath their hats, the boys in black, the men, the women—and a few of these women holding their arms out, making the sign of the cross in the direction of the dead. Among them emerged Christine; she had her hymnbook, which she held flat against her apron, hands crossed over it; she had a plaid handkerchief around her neck, with a big bow underneath her chin, like a tie. She was alone; she walked quickly. Scarcely had she gone around the church corner than Jean-Luc emerged too.

—Say! said someone, there's Jean-Luc.

—Of course, said another, he's come back up.

It was true, he had just come back up, returned to his household, after spending all winter at the bottom; he said hello to those who were there; upon which, he halted as if to speak to them, but did not speak to them, and descended toward the square. It was swarming with

22

people, as it's tradition to come there after mass to chat; the rest of the time is consumed with work, there's no time to keep in touch.

On one side are the priory and the inn, on the other, the shop that's just reopened; in the middle, a tall linden tree is planted, with a stone bench around its scaly trunk, a tree that gives the summer a beautiful round shadow, but this season looks dead. Out of habit, people stood under it, they could barely move, all of them talking, arguing, summoning one another; Jean-Luc remained there, without saying anything, his hands in his pockets.

For a first person had seen him, had come to him and said: "So, you're back?" He had said: "Yes, here I am!" And a second and a third, coming too, had said to him: "So, you're back?"; he had answered: "Yes." Then they had left him alone, because they thought: "Things aren't going well with Christine, he's not in a good mood."

But now the municipal secretary stood up on the linden tree's bench with the Commune's paperwork, silence filled the air, a large circle was formed, he began to read: "The rights holders to Biolleyres's irrigation canal are convoked into session . . . Office of Legal Proceedings and Bankruptcy . . . Bankrupt . . . Creditors . . ." Jean-Luc thought: "Why have I come back up?"

And while names followed, along with phrases and still more phrases, he felt sadness gain within him, and an overwhelming emptiness: he asked himself: "Where must I go? Must I still go home while she's there, who sneers and laughs when she sees me?" For he had not come back up on his own, she'd gone to fetch him.

At that moment someone cried out to him again: "Hey Jean-Luc!" He looked up, recognized his cousin Théodule, who shook his hand, then continued on with the others; he remained, asked himself: "What should I do?" Yet, little by little, the square emptied, soon the bells would announce noon, and people, one after another, came out of the shop with bags and parcels; he let himself go with the movement he left too, took the alley. Layers of snow, which had slid off the roofs, cut through it in certain places, all across it, mounds of snow hardened into ice; you had to go over them or else skirt them altogether by sticking close to the walls; the sky had lowered with the weight of clouds completely bound and stitched up, a child cried, chimney smoke hung in the muggy air, slackened, instead of rising up. He continued.

He halted, turned back, halted again; then took a right, went up a bit of the slope, saw the pond, his house—isolated, and turned to the north. He thought:

"It's at the world's end, why did father build here? They do say he was feral . . ."

All dressed in white on its thick layer of ice, now you could only distinguish the pond by its flat surface, whereas all around it the land went uphill and downhill, and in the back the great mountain zones of meadows and woods were hidden under fog; the house appeared there, the angle at the bottom of its walls as if cushioned and softened by snow; wedged into the slope from the back, the cellar door opening around the front to nearly scrape the ground, built of wood that was already blackened on a bedrock of stone, the uncovered roof at the top revealing large tiles of slate. And across the façade, to the side, the stairs went up, ending with a stoop, from which you entered the kitchen; from the kitchen you went on to the bedroom. And above, beneath the roof pitch, there was a second room, but it was only accessible through a ladder and a trap drilled through the floor; no one lived there, it was crammed with old things.

And yet that was enough, which is what he thought, but happiness must also reside there. When you think you will find it at home, you never go fast enough; quite the opposite, the closer he got, the more slowly he went. From afar, he already heard voices, the kitchen door having been left ajar; he felt the desire to turn back, but what was the point? He went up the stairs. He encountered Ambroisine, a friend of Christine's who had come to visit.

He was forced to speak a bit, he could hardly find the words, and Christine studied him, while Félicie, one of her sisters, sat by the fireplace. She was simple-minded, and it was impossible to guess her age, for she had a child's laugh and an old woman's wrinkles, with a wax figure and a round and hard goiter that hung around her neck, in a sort of bag of skin, like a cowbell. She had started to sing, and nodded her head while singing.

Upon which noon rang, they ate; Jean-Luc did not speak. But from time to time he looked over at his wife, and the little one, whom she held, and he asked himself: "Why do I allow it?"

He quickly finished eating: he sat near the window. At the edge of the pond, on the steep bank, children were playing, sliding and falling on top of each other, screaming and laughing; it's the age of happiness; there were three little girls in full skirts who were holding hands, halted near there, not daring to come any closer; then, on the embankment, a boy passed with a girl, going off toward Andogne, they disappeared around the bend. There was nothing else, over there, only the fog still descending, torn off by the treetops. Jean-Luc lit his pipe; once finished, he went to lie down on his bed.

He had closed the door, Christine and Ambroisine could be heard chatting, telling each other stories and repeatedly bursting into laughter; he was lying on his back, there were the dark beams of the ceiling, a low ceiling, with wooden knots and veins he let his eye travel along, and so his eye arrived at the other side of the room and the alignment of little windows, where a corner of the white meadow could be seen. Following which, his eye returned to the four or five pieces of furniture, old, his parents', which had always been there; the table covered by a white cotton rug Christine had crocheted, the two chairs, the bench, the large gray-stone frying pan, the cradle (but this was new); and the bed where he lay, and had been born, where he would probably die, a two-story bed, with a red-checkered desk he had pulled aside to lie down; then, hanging at the bedside table, the great red and blue crucifix, and a tin stoup, with a twig of juniper wood.

Chatting could still be heard from the kitchen; he vaguely looked at these things. Finally weariness came to him, he fell asleep. He woke up around four, the house was empty. He sat by the abandoned fire, which he lit back up. He warmed his feet; he packed his pipe back up.

The wind had risen, a great mountain wind that seems to come with two hands, knocking over the people on paths. As it became more and more powerful, the entire house began to crack; the door shook. And a great darkness descended from the middle of the sky, but below the horizon, through a tear in the sky, came a false light, white, which glistened on the snow, blackening the clouds that hung against the mountain, and were torn off one after another.

And Jean-Luc blew out short puffs of smoke, asked himself once more: "Why did I come back up?"

For she had come down to fetch him on two different occasions: vainly; only on the third did he follow her. And did it make any sense? Pondering this, he went back over it all: that sunny day, that afternoon; he had been renovating a path toward Anzé, working there, lifting his pickax, when she'd suddenly called him from behind a bush where she hid. He had not moved, and she, once more: "Jean-Luc!" She'd come, he had said to her: "If you're here because of me, you can be on your way!" She'd said: "It's not because of you, it's because of the little one, without whom I'll die of boredom." He had responded: "Ah! It's not because of me!" And he had been shocked, had felt his blood stir, had said: "Well then, I'll come up."

With nighttime approaching, she and he had gone to his mother's house; she had cried to her son: "If you go, you're dead to me."

However, together, they had gone up.

They had followed the path up to the roses that pierce through the snow, had found the key under the door, seen the fireplace; that was three days ago, and he still didn't understand it.

He shrugged. Here was Christine now, on her way back. Through the little windowpanes, he could see her come, walking, all bent with the child tight against her and her skirts flying all about; once at the stairs, she was forced to hold on to the railing. Then was as if thrown into the kitchen, amid a swirl of air that abruptly put out the flame in the fireplace, and everything disappeared in smoke. She put the child down at one end of the bench, she undid the scarf tied firmly beneath her chin.

—It's blowing hard out there! she said. Poor Ambroisine will have a hard time going down.

And then:

—You're still sulking!

28

Next, touching her head:

—Yours is very hard, you know!

He remained despondent and closed off, the evening came, they ate again, the night fully arrived; when it was time to go to bed, she said to him: "Are you coming?" He said: "You go ahead!" He waited a while. Then, he pushed the door, he made sure Christine was asleep, and only then did he slide into bed. He did everything slowly, to ensure she wouldn't wake; he lay down next to her, but could not fall asleep.

The candle burned on the table with its little pointed flame, slightly smoky at the tip. And he saw her there so near, whom he had so loved; her loose braids hung on the pillow; from which came out her little ear and, pulled back, her forehead was smooth and glowing; ah! he would have liked to plant a kiss on it, but he contained himself; and then, because in dreaming she had taken out her bare arm, he couldn't stop himself, he stretched out his hand, but almost at once pulled it back, as if burned by that touch; he began to shiver, he blew out the candle.

Are you so weak?—that's what he asked himself; and he searched for sleep, but was long in finding it; the night's hours, counted by the church tower and its big voice, passed one by one, through the wind that kept rising then falling in waves on the roof, and so its sound covered everything; then there was an interval of silence, the cracks of the ceiling beams sounded.

The following days, having harnessed the sled to his cow Foumette (which means "color of smoke"), he took care of spreading the manure. Because Foumette was in calf, she only barely fit into the shaft. He pushed her back, he fixed her in place with the tight ropes; upon which, he cried: "Giddy up!" and they left, he and his beast.

There was still fog, but it stopped right at the edge of the flat land around the village, and you entered it like you enter a door that shuts the moment it's opened. And Foumette, neck outstretched, pulled through the path of melting mud; Jean-Luc walking by the cow's side at a slow pace, leaning forward, the rope of his whip placed around her neck, the handle that beat against his pants. He had put on a worn felt hat with lowered edges, his jacket had holes through the elbows, his gray shirt showed his neck with the prominent bulge.

In one place, a little above the pond, he left the path and started up the slope sideways. There, the layer of snow was still thick. Foumette's short legs sank in, while the sled began to tilt under the broad weight, and, in the great silence, the wooden steel-tipped ice skates whistled. Jean-Luc cried: "Giddy up, Foumette!" and cracked his whip.

And, at times, during a sunny spell, lower toward the village, or higher up toward the slopes, other men who worked like him appeared with their little carts, then everything was covered up once more and disappeared.

And so Jean-Luc, digging his pitchfork into the load,

spread it in even piles on the surface of the piece of the meadow he owned, a very small piece as they usually are in the region, and still split everywhere, due to too much sharing of the land; he made his piles. Then, his sled emptied, he headed back.

But often, he rested a moment, standing next to Foumette, and at the bottom he looked at his house, now exposed and all diminished in the nook; beneath the window some pink washing dried, the door was shut, the chimney smoked; once again he thought: "I've come back up!" Once again he asked himself why.

To which he answered: "Because of the property, which still has to be taken care of regardless." But he felt that he was lying to himself. "Because of the little one." Yet he thought: "It would be better for him not to have a mother at all than to have this one." "No," he went on, "it's because of what she said, I felt anger." There was pride in him. And so, going deeper, to where one hardly dares to look: "Could it be that I need her?" But he stiffened immediately: "Never!" he said. "I came back, what's done is done and I'll work for her and she for me, and we'll live together, but as for forgiving her . . ." He repeated: "Never!"

He went on looking at the house where he had been happy, for under that little roof two hearts had fully given themselves, and the door, at night, shuts on the day's contentment for the nighttime kiss, and you are broken with weariness, but you think to yourself: "I do have a little wife, that's the poor man's pleasure, and she's rather attached to me."

He shook his head, and went back the way he came, now sitting on the sled and making his way little by little. He didn't stop working until nighttime, looking to forget through weariness, the way others do through wine. Raising his hat, he scratched the back of his neck; and back home, kept quiet and smoked, spitting on the hot ash where the dark embers sat whistling. Outwardly his life had remained the same, with Félicie who came and sat in the same place the entire day, nodding her head and singing her songs; and old Simon, Christine's father, who sometimes came; all contorted and paralyzed, leaning on his large cane like a tree on its stake, wearing a blue frock coat with tails and copper buttons from bygone days; and, while he traveled from his house to his son-in-law's, the sundial's gnomon nearly had the time to move from one digit to another.

The wind had picked up again, warmer, the wind called the snow-eater; the dark layers widened; the pond blackened, cracked: one day the water was liberated. And so the dead frogs floated back up from the bottom, and the murders of crows flew in circles around them. The shadows arrived; there was the forest's darkness, a blue-black on the mountain, a sky that remained burdened, and some scattered islands of light. Again, she called him. But he answered her: "Never."

CHAPTER III

YET, AT THE END OF APRIL, he broke his leg.

On account of early snow the previous fall, they hadn't been able to finish chopping wood in Sassette, and they'd gone back there, Théodule Chabbey, old Romain Aymon, Jean-Pierre Carraux, and Fardet—Jean-Luc was the fifth. It is in the gorge of La Zaut behind Le Bourni, a steep and rocky slope that runs straight down to the flowing torrent, full in this season.

At a very early hour, they had already started their drudgery; the fir trees in question had bent over the void on their own as a result of the weight of the branches up top, there was no need to tie the rope, the men attacked them at the root; when the notch was deep enough, they broke, smashing on the rockery, bouncing all the way to the path.

There was still fog. It had taken shape little by little, rising from the bottom of the gorge like water does in a basin. Strangled between boulders, the great rumble of water filled the air; the men could hardly hear one another. There they were, hanging on the slope:

then, a little farther ahead, it steepens some more, and suddenly, it becomes a real wall, a hundred-meter wall. Where the bisse runs, a great wooden canal suspended in the air, fixed with beams dug into cracks in the rock, thus reaching the length of the wall up to the areas of lingering snow, from which it gathers the water that serves to irrigate meadows; without which, the climate is too dry, the grass would burn quickly. You see it shrink, still overhanging the void, now like a string, marked in black against the lighter stone, then suddenly turn, disappear.

They worked all morning; around noon they ate; following which, they immediately took up their axes again, for work was calling. Nonetheless, around three, they found themselves rather ahead, as only one out of the five trees they had to chop down still stood standing, the largest one, yes, but old and rotten; and Théodule had started on it, while under him, Jean-Luc and Romain had begun to limb the tree. Neither of them spoke, too busy, and out of breath too; due to habit and the way it forms, the men no longer even heard the great sound of the water, it was turned into silence; nothing but the axes chopping away, the larger strokes, Théodule's on the fly, and the other shorter and sharper hacks of Jean-Luc and Romain.

The sun had lowered in the sky; suddenly it pierced through the clouds, the large side of the bisse turned pink; somewhere water dripped, there was a damp layer, it shone like gold.

Smoke was rising from the hills, and, far away, at the bottom of the great valley, the vast land came into view, with the river's silver bar and at the back of the horizon, a heap of tall mountains. A great bird of prey appeared and hung in the air for a moment; then it fell like a stone.

A small warm wind had blown in, vapors passed, rising then coming undone, much like fine wisps of ink in the fallen light, where the sun had drowned. You could already smell the damp scent of the evening.

You could still hear the axe hacking away at the heart of the tree, Théodule lifting the tool with the long handle, swinging it forward with a rounded movement of the shoulders; the shiny iron bouncing out of the widening notch. Suddenly the trunk cracked. Théodule cried: "Watch out!", then began to strike again; the tip of the fir tree shook. "Watch out!" Théodule cried once more. But his mouth was still wide open when the trunk showed something like hesitation; it leaned to the right, it leaned to the left, and Théodule barely had enough time to leap back: the entire mass fell, among the whistling of branches, collapsed and rolled in a sort of pine needle smoke as bark debris launched into the air around him; then, all of a sudden, Romain, who had hidden behind a large rock, came running, screaming: "Ah! My God! he's trapped underneath." And those who were still on the path climbed the slope in great haste.

Jean-Luc was indeed lying there, having been trapped during his escape. His bottom half was trapped, so that only his top half showed, with a face like the white of bread, and wide-open misty eyes. The forehead's skin was split open, blood had trickled down to his mustache; his chest was bare. And did not stir, flat on his back, arms far apart, like those of a man nailed in the shape of a cross.

So that at first they thought he was dead, and Romain, who was pious, crossing himself, said a prayer, as they observed from his moving lips, while the others remained standing there, filled only with great astonishment. Then Fardet removed his hat and said twice: "Hell! Hell!" Théodule, behind his large black beard, had grown even paler than Jean-Luc; he said: "I did cry out, only the trunk was rotten at its core."

But suddenly Jean-Luc let out a sigh, the red color of blood creeping back under his skin, he looked around him, most likely remembered everything; he said: "It's nothing, only my legs are trapped."

They pulled him out from where he was, they laid him out on a flat mossy surface, they placed a garment rolled up in the form of a pillow under his head, and, because Romain had gone to get the small keg, the wine finished warming him and helped him to regain his senses. Then they examined how hurt he was; along with his shirt, his pants had been ripped to bits, and, though one of his legs was only scratched and bruised, when they touched the other, he groaned. Below the calf, the bone had broken, so that it was already very swollen, and, on one side, a black blood clot hung from the wound.

"It's nothing!" repeated Jean-Luc, for he was courageous. Upon which Romain said to him: "Take another swig." Jean-Luc drank. The four of them lifted him up, they carried him to the path.

Having made a kind of stretcher with branches and rope, they laid him down on it, then were off. Romain had taken the lead. The others slowly followed the path that borders the gorge, which goes on widening, then opens up, and you arrive in the meadows; then the village appears.

She had come to meet him, and, as soon as she saw a speck in the distance, ran, just as Romain had found her, her sleeves rolled up, her apron soaked (for she'd been doing the dishes and had left in a hurry)—she started to run from afar, and arrived, throwing herself at him: "What's wrong? she said, what's wrong?" For she feared that Romain hadn't told her the truth. Jean-Luc answered her: "I've broken my leg." Then she kissed him in front of everyone, many people having already come; she repeated: "Is that really the truth? the truth? and this blood!" And she wiped this blood, with her handkerchief, then went off toward the house; and when the men arrived with the stretcher, the bed was already made, the water on the fire, the cloth for the bandages all prepared. Then, as soon as Jean-Luc was in bed, she sat near him.

But he didn't seem to see her, having closed his eyes, nor to hear her when she spoke, and she seemed to resign herself, no longer moving, no longer speaking. Marie and her husband, the blacksmith, had come, then some neighbors, the whole kitchen was full; people came in and out continuously; someone had gone to fetch the butcher, for he was an expert in such things. He cleaned the forehead and leg wounds, he said: "The doctor has to come."

Christine immediately burst into tears. Théodule had already harnessed the mule, then had gone; she remained there, her head down, crossing both hands over her face, tears rolling through her fingers one by one; and Marie said to her: "Calm down Christine, it won't be serious!" but she kept crying. Then, once in a while, she would start up again: "Jean-Luc, listen to me! Jean-Luc, listen to me!" He didn't even turn his head.

This made her cry even harder; then suddenly her tears dried, she said to Marie: "Have you made some tea?" And because she answered no: "Look, the fever's taking hold of him." Christine ran to the kitchen and made some tea, which she brought him, but he didn't want to drink it. And from that moment on, she no longer left her chair until late in the evening when the doctor arrived, and Jean-Luc began to writhe and uncover himself.

The doctor, having entered, placed his case on the table, he examined the swelling: "What I need," he said, "is two strong men." The blacksmith left; and the doctor, once again, addressing Christine: "You'll have to leave too." But she didn't want to. He added: "Then you'll remain calm!" She sat watching him, meanwhile two men had arrived. And like the doctor had ordered, they took Jean-Luc by the shoulders, while, with the help of the blacksmith, the doctor began to pull on the leg. It was extremely swollen, shapeless, the foot all round and purple; they pulled on it with all their might. Jean-Luc let out a great scream.

And he continued to scream despite his courage, the pain was so sharp; the stronger the men pulled, the bone still resisting, the more piercing the screams became. The doctor said to him: "It's almost done, be patient!" and Jean-Luc clung to his chair, gritting his teeth, it was all in vain.

In the meantime Christine had walked over to a corner of the room. At the first sound of his screams, a great shiver had seized her, and she'd plugged her ears, but it was no use, she still heard them, those screams, as if from within, they shook all of her—and so, suddenly, she threw herself at the doctor.

No one had time to stop her. She was yelling: "Let him go! let him go, I tell you, you're going to kill him." She had him by the shoulders; as she was very strong, he couldn't get rid of her. "Get her out of here," he said, "she's crazy!" It wasn't easy, the blacksmith had to let go of Jean-Luc, and attempt to drag Christine to the door. She struggled with him, the doctor was saying: "Hurry up now!"

But, at that instant, Jean-Luc spoke: "Pierre-François, be gentle." And he started again: "Leave the room, Christine, they say it's almost done, you can return

39

afterward." She was looking at him, and he was looking at her. "Poor woman," he continued, "her heart aches to see me suffer!" And abruptly she had become docile, she said to François: "I'll leave on my own," and indeed left, entering the kitchen where Marie waited for her, while the doctor went back to his task, which was soon brought to completion.

She came right away; while the doctor had gone to wash his hands, and the men to drink, you could hear her saying to Jean-Luc: "Is it possible? You still love me a little!" And Jean-Luc answering her.

So that when Marie, having finished putting everything away, wished to say goodnight to them, she knocked out of discretion: no one answered; she pushed the door open. Christine was lying at Jean-Luc's side.

She hadn't wanted anyone's help in watching over him. She was lying there, lying with all of her clothes on, sprawled out near her husband, gently running her hand through his hair—and he had his eyes closed beneath her caresses. She was repeating: "Say, are you alright, big fellow?" He answered: "Yes, thanks." She kissed him, he returned her kiss. And, stirring, writhing in his bed, with the heavy leg that made him suffer, at times he was carried off by some kind of nightmare; but, returning to himself, he found her there, with her fresh hands and bright smile.

Time passed, she hadn't left him. You could hear the great hours of the night crack, fall, tumbling from the church tower like ripe fruits shaken off; nothing but the little light, and Jean-Luc lying down, and Christine at his side. He had nodded off, his head on his arm; through the misty little windows, you could see a corner of the pond; everything was in silence.

Yet Jean-Luc started to writhe again. Suddenly, as midnight rang with its twelve sluggish chimes, he woke with a jolt, he asked Christine: "Are they ringing for the dead?" "Ah! my God! What were you thinking about? she said. Jean-Luc! Listen, I'm here." And pulling him close to her, she laid her cheek against his prickly cheek; he had calmed down at once, at once he fell back asleep.

Jean-Luc healed quickly, robust as he was; the swelling had gone down, they put a cast on him; soon he was rid of those awful feverish nights.

It was a clear morning. He had slept in, beautiful sunlight filtered in through the window, the grass had already turned green again, and now Christine arrived, bringing the little Henri, who was beginning to speak and get to know him; she said to him: "That's your Papa there." He repeated: "Papa! Papa!" Jean-Luc extended his arms to him.

She gave him the child to hold for a moment while she went to make coffee, then, having returned with a full cup, she took the little one again and held him under both arms while he attempted to walk, for he too was beginning to walk, but first she had to pull up the long swaddling clothes and, in an amusing manner, he launched forward his little feet, with their large pink wool stockings, advancing hunched over, wobbling, while Christine, who had lowered herself, walked behind him; then from time to time she extended her arms and the little one took two or three steps on his own. "You see, he's got it!" she'd say, but at that instant, he would fall forward; she barely had time to catch him.

She turned toward the bed; she saw Jean-Luc, who held his cup and had ceased drinking, sitting against the pillows, watching her and the child. She said to him:

—He's so beautiful and strong for his age!

He said: "Oh yes!" and she, coming closer, threw the little one over to him, saying: "Go see your Papa." And while the child rolled against him, Jean-Luc laughed in his short beard, which had grown back. He said to Christine: "You come too." She said to him: "What about your leg?" "Don't worry," he said, "I can't feel the pain anymore." She came too.

He spoke to her, he said: "Listen, it's all been forgotten, right?" "Of course." And he, once more: "Of course?" "As much as I can!" she said. And then, she said, "Kiss me." "And where would you like me to kiss you?"

She smiled, looking at him with her face right up to his; at the same time, she lifted her hair, two pretty folds against her tanned cheeks. Between her parted lips, her beautiful white teeth gleamed; one of them, on the side, had had no room to grow, and remained a little crooked; she said to him:

—Kiss me on the light of my eyes.

She stretched them out to him, they were damp and beautiful, the color of chestnuts; he held them wide open beneath him.

She went on:

—And now, on the forehead.

He kissed her on the forehead, hers was high and rounded.

—Christine, he said, little Christine!

But she was saying: "And now on my cheeks!" And he bit into them like apples. And then she laughed: "Some more," she said, "as much as you can and under my nose."

Only, as she looked up, he had already grabbed her, pressed her against him, and lifted her with the little one holding on to her; and he could see now his old love had returned, as great as before, even greater, as if the days of their separation and the difficult things that had come to pass had been destroyed and flattened between them. And he was delighted by his broken leg, by the day in Sassette, by his pain, by everything. Which is why he called her sweet names, speaking to her from within his kiss:

—Christine, Christine my love, how cool one feels against these teeth.

She said to him:

—Maybe they're to bite!

He kissed her again. Little birds cried along the edge of the roof.

CHAPTER IV

HAPPINESS REIGNED ONCE MORE. He'd bought her some fabric for a dress, which she tailored and sewed herself, having borrowed the machine from a neighbor; he, stretching out his leg on the bench, watched her spin the wheel with the bouncing needle, while Marie gave her advice.

Then he started to go out a little, leaning on his cane; he had hired a man to work the land during the day; he went to keep an eye on him, he returned, he had a brand new heart, a brand new head.

Spring had arrived, mingled as it is of blue and black, with days of beautiful sunshine, then some showers and some wind. But what did it matter to him?—he found pleasure in the rain, he found pleasure in the sun. There had been the violet anemones, the crocus that loves water, the hepatica of the hedges, the primrose like plates. Then come the gentians. You feel like you can see the wheat growing: suddenly, it's one foot tall. And, at night, the air that comes through tastes like fresh bread. Jean-Luc opened his mouth, he said: "How nice!"

Then he found her, who had heard him come from afar, who came out on the doorstep, who said: "Do you want me to help you climb the stairs?"

He answered: "I can do it well enough on my own."

He demonstrated how well he could.

"I feel like I'm sixteen years old!" he said; then other little footsteps and another little voice sounded, it was Henri, who arrived behind his mother; Jean-Luc would toss him in the air; and the little Henri laughed and was afraid at once.

Likewise the people who had kept their distance began to reappear Sundays after mass, some neighbors, Christine's friends; little by little too, Jean-Luc walked with more ease, he went through the village; someone would invite him in for a drink, he would enter; and in turn he would invite others, and they came. One night, there were about seven or eight people in the cellar, Christine and Marie too. They had gone for the muscat, Jean-Luc filled the glass, the men passed it to each other, standing in a circle around the barrel. And Christine was in a corner, from which she chatted and joked, but the others knew how to respond—and they laughed about Marie, who hid both hands under her apron every time you held out a glass to her.

—I'm a good drinker! said Christine.

She did what she said; the others did like her. Pierre Carre appeared, with his mule. He was a big man, always drunk, who spent his life on the trails; and, if in the morning there was a chance he still led his beast, at night it was always his beast that led him. They called him, he came, but didn't enter; he couldn't have, he remained at the doorstep, leaning his back on the mule's packsaddle; they said to him: "Where are you coming from?", he lifted his arm in the air: "From over there!" for he didn't know anymore, in the haze of it all.

Then Jean-Luc, pouring him a drink:

—You need this one to make all the others go down.

He answered:

—Definitely! I feel empty up top.

He repeated:

—The bottom is fine, it's the top that isn't.

Following which everyone burst into laughter, and the voices carried far into the night that was coming, while Carre had gone again, once more hanging on to the tail of his beast, barely staying within the edges of the trail.

Someone cried to him again: "Just be patient, we'll find a way to widen it some more." Then everyone returned to the cellar; other neighbors had come; from the board where it's kept, they'd been to fetch a quarter of cheese; they ate, they drank again, the stories flowed; Sergeant Braillard was there, who was the town's biggest boaster, and the funniest thing was that he believed his own fibs when he'd been drinking. They said to him: "Tell us the one about the Bear."

In the mountain there was a pass called Le Pas de l'Ours. The Sergeant began: "I was walking over that way, I see the bear coming; I take my knife out of my pocket, I halt, it comes forward, I was thinking: it's going to attack me, but I'll know how to defend myself; not at all, it stands upright on its paws then, it puts its hand on my shoulder and says to me: "'Sergeant Braillard . . . !'"

He couldn't go on, they were laughing too much, and Christine's apron, from the way she had bitten it to stop herself from laughing, was all chewed up at the bottom: only the Sergeant remained serious, watching the others with a wounded air.

It was late when they parted ways. Night had fully arrived. It was hot and mild, with, at the top of the mountains, beneath the light of the stars, the great snow that glittered, but everywhere at the bottom the flowers and the smell, and the hay already ripening; as they went up the stairs, Jean-Luc had placed his arm around Christine's waist; there was a crescent moon in the sky, it slid among the clouds like a little pointed boat.

And so, his leg stronger, Jean-Luc had been able to start working again. It was the start of the summer, he worked with joy, out of desire and love for her. And when, one day, someone (for there are always people who take pleasure in doing harm), when one day someone said to him: "You know, Augustin is back!" he answered:

—What do I care?

He left in the morning, he returned at noon; then, gone once again, they didn't see him until nighttime; sometimes, Christine accompanied him to the fields, but ordinarily she stayed home to milk and prepare the meal, with, in addition, the little one to care for. When he returned late, his great pleasure was, from the bend in the path, to glimpse the little light in the kitchen window—and this open door too, this red square in the night where a black shape would appear; and so he thought: "It's her, she's waiting for me."

And so time passed with such haste that it seemed the days had diminished by a good half; in such a way that you look back with regret, but ahead of you there seem to be promises, and the two combined still make for happiness. And Jean-Luc told himself: "It will last forever."

He was mistaken, you place your trust in something this way, but much like a rotten board, it snaps beneath your foot. One night, he didn't see the little light, Christine had gone out; two days later likewise; once, having come back in the middle of the afternoon, he found the door shut; he asked Christine: "Where have you been?" She told him: "To the store, then to the baker's"; but he couldn't stop himself from thinking: "In the past, she went out less, she was always here."

Yet she was gay like before, thoughtful; it was underneath that he felt she was changed, she was undoing herself from him. With her same eyes, her same voice, dressed in identical fashion, and the same words in her mouth, she was different, as he thought—and the more time went on, the more she changed. Perhaps a little less patient, more nervous, more distracted. He asked her: "What's wrong with you?" She answered: "Nothing, what do you want there to be wrong with me?" And as he continued: "There's something!" she laughed, she said: "You're imagining things!"

And so inside him: "Perhaps I'm mistaken." But the weeks advancing, he was made to believe he was not. He would go to bed very early, rising at daybreak—meanwhile Christine would undress the child, then return to the kitchen; closing his eyes, he would hear her coming and going, he fell asleep to this sound of footsteps.

It's the hour where the village too goes to sleep. The angelus has rung; at the fountain one or two more cows, driven along the path, come to drink; a boy returning from the bottom walks behind his wagon, humming an air on his harmonica; the lanterns come and go, glimmering upon the house walls; then the doors are shut and fall back on silence, with nothing left but the little lamps like eyes inside the night, closing one after the other.

One night, when the little one had woken him with his cries, he found himself alone in the bed; he listened: no one. Yet it was ten thirty; he waited; a moment later, she came home; he asked her: "Where are you coming from?" She said: "Félicie came to get me, Father wasn't well."

He didn't say any more, she lay near him and at once fell asleep. But he thought, this time with self-assurance: "Something's wrong with her." For several days, he sought what it was, without finding it. Was she still sore at him? for grudges come and go—but what about the day in Sassette? Or else had he made her sad without meaning to?—but when and how? he didn't know. He kept searching.

On one of those days, from afar, he saw Augustin coming up the village street. And, as soon as he saw Jean-Luc, he turned his back to him, went back the way he came. Then Jean-Luc had an idea: "I know what it is . . . She probably still cares for him, and she's angry to see us quarreling."

He just had to wait for the right occasion, which soon arose. He'd been to the shop; Augustin was just leaving. He went straight up to Augustin, he said to him: "Hey, Augustin!" and held out his hand, which the latter took, despite his surprise.

—Listen, I've been thinking, we have to be good friends again, that's why I've come, and if you'd like that, well, it's been decided.

—Haven't we always been good friends? said Augustin.

He was a handsome tall man with a red face, always well-dressed, with a black hat pushed back, a silver pocket watch and a collar; he worked in hotels, as they say; and so he was absent seven months out of the year (having left the previous winter nearly the same time as Jean-Luc), then he returned for two or three months, went back to running his property.

Jean-Luc continued:

—But, for us to be quite sure, you have to come over and have a drink.

And just as Augustin answered: "Another time," "Listen," Jean-Luc went on, "I think to myself: If you don't come, it's because there's still something between us; and if there's nothing there then you'll come, and we'll have that drink."

So convincingly that Augustin gave in and said:

"Fine then," without understanding, and the two of them left together. While they walked, Jean-Luc thought: "She'll be trapped, alright!" In front of the house, he cried: "Hey! Christine!" She appeared on the stoop. He, from below: "Christine, there's two of us, go and fetch something to drink."

It was already dark, she couldn't see anything at first. Then, as he went up the stairs, she recognized Augustin; she moved back without saying anything, she grew pale, next a blush appeared; she looked at her husband. He was saying to her: "Will you invite us in?" She made an effort and responded: "It's just that we don't have anything good to drink here." He said to her: "Fetch it anyway, it's to toast our friendship." She went on: "You're not coming down?" "No, said Jean-Luc, we'll be more comfortable in the kitchen."

She went to fetch the wine from the cellar, and, having come back up, found Jean-Luc and Augustin already sitting down, Jean-Luc packing his pipe, his tobacco in front of him, which he handed to him, saying: "Have a taste, it's a new kind they gave me to try."

And Augustin took the pack, while Jean-Luc filled the glasses. There were only two.

He called: "Christine!" She was already gone, she replied from the bedroom: "What do you want?" "What about your glass?" From behind the half-shut door: "I don't want any, I'm not thirsty." "What are you doing?" "I'm putting the little one's clothes in order." "Hurry up," he said, "we're bored without you."

She had gone to sit in a dark corner, and no longer moved. She listened to the two men talk, first with sparse phrases, which then came to life little by little, the carafe (it was a tin pitcher) being full, Augustin speaking of his positions, the hotels he'd been to, Jean-Luc saying: "How much do you earn?" and he responding: "Sometimes a hundred francs." "Per month!" "Per month." "That much!", then came a silence, Augustin added: "But it's a short season."

They went on speaking, she thought: "He's brought him over? Is it even possible?" But once again Jean-Luc's voice rose: "Christine!" "Argh!" she said. "Are you not finished?" "Not yet." At that moment, he entered: "What are you doing? It looks like you're sulking." And, before she could even turn around, he'd grabbed her by the arm and, holding her firmly, brought her over, grabbed a glass as he went by, put it down in front of her, made her sit near Augustin:

—This is how it's done! he said.

All at once her countenance changed:

—I was worried I'd bore you, but if you'll have me . . .

And as Jean-Luc was laughing again, she began to laugh too. "We're good friends," he said. "Of course!" she said, "cheers to both." She drank, the other two drank.

She was gay, they were gay, and at first Augustin had seemed a little embarrassed, but the embarrassment quickly passed. She had opened the drawer with the old deck of cards, she had said: "Shall we play?", and the other two wanting to play, she shuffled the deck.

They raised an arm, they laid down their cards; the lantern gave light, there at the end of the table, with the carafe and its open lid, its gray tin belly and the gleaming yellow glasses. Christine grabbed hers again. "Ah! you're drinking," said Jean-Luc. "You didn't want to, a moment ago. That's women for you!" "And men, what are men like?" Christine started up again.

And Augustin became bolder: "Don't you know?" She looked at him at length.

They had started to play again, in the little window-panes she had seen the gray color change, darken, turning sapphire; Jean-Luc was happy.

—Maybe so, he continued, but what I know best, is that we were foolish not to see each other, right Augustin?

—We were foolish, the both of us.

Jean-Luc was winning, he held the most declarations. "Diamond trump!" he said. "And now pinochle, two at a time!" They trumped. "My turn, and my turn again!" And, writing down the points, he added them up on a piece of paper.

—Me again! he said.

Christine responded:

—Lucky in cards, unlucky in love.

He just laughed. And their voices sounded one after another, their requests, their answers, the names of the cards they threw, a number: "Trump!" "I'll trump." "I'll deal the cards," and meanwhile Christine looked at Augustin, who was leaning into her. They were very close to each other, facing Jean-Luc who sat across from them. Then throwing her cards down: "I've had enough," she said, "let's play something else."

She stood up, went to fetch her scarf from the nail, a white cotton scarf with embroidered red flowers, walked back over to Jean-Luc: "Turn around!" "What for?" "Turn some more!" To please her, Jean-Luc had turned around.

Then she said to him:

—I'll put it on you, who sees so clearly.

And she blindfolded him. It's a game played by children; the one with the blindfold has to seek; if he catches someone, he has to guess who it is.

The scarf was big, folded over; Jean-Luc's face was covered, and, a little surprised, he stood there blindfolded. "But we're only three!" "What does it matter," she said, "we're having fun, we're passing the time . . . You promise

55

you can't see anything?" "Nothing at all." "Sure, very sure?" She stuck out her tongue at him.

Augustin muffled his laugh; as for Christine, she laughed out loud; and meanwhile Jean-Luc having started to seek, they both escaped him, running around the kitchen. He walked, his arms outstretched; he banged into the hayrack, he banged into the table, the others laughed every time, he continued anyway, he turned, and depending on whether he got closer or farther away, Christine cried to him: "Hot! . . . Cold!" or else: "You're burning hot!" and he, sensing her near, would throw himself in her direction, but she moved aside, and he would crash into the wall.

He halted and said:

—It's too hard, there aren't enough people.

—Dummy, she said, speed up!

And just at that moment, finding herself near Augustin at the other end of the kitchen, she embraced him, so that he kissed her, and she allowed it. And meanwhile Jean-Luc, like she'd asked for, had started to spin faster; the whip hanging on the door fell, a stool fell, he tripped on the table, which he then dragged behind him, the others still escaping; it was no use, he was excited by the game, this sound of footsteps fleeing him, the brush of Christine's skirts, and suddenly, having touched her arm, he cried: "I caught you!" But she said: "That's not true, you have to knock on my back three times."

He started again; and then he halted once more,

out of breath. This time, everything was quiet, he said: "Where are you?" No response. He said again: "You're not allowed to hide!" Still no response. Then something like a scurry of footsteps sounded by the door, the lock clicked, he went on: "What are you doing?" Then the door opened (as he understood through the sound of water outside), he thought: "They're leaving!", he lifted his scarf. But at that same moment Christine cried to him: "You're cheating, you're cheating!", his hands fell back down; so he heard footsteps on the stoop, then down the stairs; and he continued to follow them. By groping around, he arrived at the door, then, holding on to the rail, it was his turn to go down the steps.

He found himself on the path; Christine was already gone. She had said to Augustin: "Come with me," and had dragged him away. A little to the side there's a barn, they had gone to hide behind the barn; they waited a moment, then suddenly Christine went to look. Jean-Luc hadn't moved from where he stood. Above the boulders the moon began to rise, a great red moon, with a round forehead and a round skull—and, as if a great weight was holding it back, it rose dramatically into the sky. Its empty eyes came first, then its flat nose, then its hollow mouth; a fine silver light, like a powder shaken out, began to fall through the air, and trembled.

And Jean-Luc was still on the path, her scarf in his hands. He saw Christine pop her head around the corner of the barn then abruptly duck it back in; he called:

"Christine!" She didn't move, he called once again. She answered: "Come find us!" But, now in a changed voice, he cried louder: "Come back or I'm locking the door!" So she showed herself, and, behind her, Augustin. Jean-Luc hadn't waited for her; he was already going back up the stairs.

—What's wrong with him? said Augustin.

—How do I know? she said.

And then:

—I have to go. Kiss me one more time.

Which he did, and she, having left him, headed home. She found Jean-Luc leaning on his elbows at the table. Hearing her enter, he didn't lift his head, he kept it down, his eyes facing down too, with a crease between his eyes. She asked him:

—What's going on?

—What's going on, he answered, is that you're making a fool of me.

—Me, making a fool of you!

She went on:

—Don't you understand we're having fun? We're gay, you see! We're having fun! We're gay, we go and hide, you come and find us . . . And then, when there isn't enough room to hide . . . And who was it that brought Augustin here, you big jealous man?

He said:

—Things seem rather clear.

She was now leaning into him, resting on his

shoulder, and at first he moved away from her; but, coming even closer and holding him with the arm she'd placed around his neck, suddenly she said to him: "You know, I have a secret."

He asked her: "What secret?" "Ah," she said, "you have to be good, otherwise I won't tell you a thing!" And because she felt that he was already giving in: "Give me your big ear." And then, from up close: "I think I'm pregnant again."

He couldn't believe it.

—Since when?

—Since just now.

And, that night, he was happy once more, he even regretted having been angry.

Then came other nights, filled with worry. And he kept an eye on her, but she was clever. He tortured himself, he wasn't sure of a thing anymore. Finally came this last evening.

CHAPTER V

HE STRETCHED HIS ARM ACROSS the bed, seeking the warm spot and the shape of her body lying down; he found emptiness. He opened his eyes little by little, he looked around, all was dark. He looked around and thought: "Am I dreaming or am I awake?"

A cold and faint feeling came over his entire body, with a buzzing in his head; his shoulders weighed a great deal on the straw mattress. The hour rang, he counted the strokes, there were eleven; it sounded for the second time, he counted the strokes once more. He said: "Eleven o'clock, eleven o'clock at night! Things are going to change around here."

Outside there was a clear gray light, from which the windows cut themselves like slabs of zinc. He remained without moving, he lifted his head, which came right back down. A mouse ran around upstairs. He heard it come, with its abrupt scampering, then a gnawing and a nibbling, to which a breath of wind at one corner of the roof responded, and then passed, and everything was quiet. He thought: "The wind is rising, because of the rain, and the weather is mild."

Suddenly, little Henri called to him. This made him fully regain consciousness. He saw his room, the furniture, things as they were. He said: "My name is Jean-Luc Robille, my wife is Christine Geindre." He left bed, went to the cradle, took the little one, returned, laid him down on the side of the wall.

And already, feeling the pleasant heat of a human presence, the child hushed, having rested his head on his father's shoulder, and his little body loosened with the abandon of sleep. He sighed once more, seeking a warm spot on the sheets, then, tightening his fists against his face, fell back asleep.

But Jean-Luc kept vigil, for his thoughts were now clear within him and clear was his resolution. He thought to himself: "She's already cheated on me once, this is the second time. I was a coward before, will I be a coward once more?" He answered himself: "No!" And a crease formed between his two eyes, for he was ashamed of himself.

He hadn't turned on the lamp, darkness reigned, with only the pale gleam of the small windowpanes, which projected onto a corner of the table, and the rest of the furniture was barely visible; he was lying on his back, the little one's breath sounded. Time passed.

Then there was the sound of footsteps on the stairs, but a muffled sound, as if someone was walking on tiptoe. Following which, the kitchen door was opened, it didn't squeak; Jean-Luc thought: "She must have oiled it."

He remained on his back, he didn't move in the least: nor did he move when the lock clicked, and it was only when he heard the sound of full skirts skimming the floor that he realized someone had entered. Next someone halted as if to listen, then the footsteps started up again, advancing halfway through the room, and at that moment Christine stood before him.

She set her brooch on the table, she came to the bed. He hadn't closed his eyes, he kept them locked in her direction; she didn't notice. She had started to undress. She placed her camisole and her half-slip on the chair very slowly; lifting her arms, she removed the comb from inside her chignon, then she went to lie down; but, just as she was leaning one knee on the edge of the bed, suddenly she was caught, having met his gaze. It was calm, as if empty, and solely fixed on her; under this gaze, however, she no longer moved, remaining there, one knee up.

He said to her:

—You're very late.

His voice, too, was calm, not the voice of a man woken with a jolt, but of someone who has waited and kept vigil, which frightened her more.

She could not find an answer; Jean-Luc went on:

—Is it because you have trouble sleeping that you're going to bed so late?

Precisely then, midnight rang. She said:

—You see, my father's ill again; he needed me.

He said:

63

—Ah! He's ill!

—His paralysis has gotten hold of him again, his heavy leg . . .

But he, interrupting her:

—You can't stop lying!

And at once:

—Swear it!

She answered:

—I swear!

He sat up, he turned the lamp back on, he came down from the bed, and went to the door to lock it. And she had moved away from him, taken with fright, her strength down all of a sudden. The crucifix was on the wall, Jean-Luc set it down on the table. He came to her; she had hidden her face behind the fold of her arm; he took her by this arm, she allowed it.

He brought her before the crucifix and, having released her arm, took her hand, which he placed on the crucifix, and lowering his voice once more because of the child:

—You swore it, swear it one more time!

She had turned her head the other way and, using all of her body weight, she was leaning to one side, sought to escape; but he tightened his grip around her wrist, with such force that tears formed in her eyes. Yet she did not swear, because of the Christ placed before her, whose name she bore. And, all of her blood having descended to her heart, with her waist already heavy, she was sad and miserable, leaning back, and yet attempting to stand straight again, with still some pride deep within her, while she suffered the humiliation.

But he had started up again:

—Swear that you're not coming from his.

Then came a moment of hesitation, and the crucifix sat there. It was an old crucifix, the kind that you can stand upright, with a pedestal fully carved in wood; it was painted red and blue, with ornaments and a very small Christ, and the arms of the cross very large; the crucifix also seemed to be waiting.

And Jean-Luc watched Christine, and now she watched him, too, with glittering eyes, even feverish, and at that instant a kind of mockery shone through them, so that without even meaning to he tightened his grip again, and she writhed in pain. He spoke in a rushed tone:

—And the little one, is he mine?

This time, at once, she answered:

—I swear!

—And the one who isn't born yet?

She looked down:

—I don't know.

And so, as if despite himself, he violently pushed her back, she fell against the wall, tears ran down her cheeks one by one, rolling down to her shirt, under which she was naked and numb with cold; he crouched against her, still holding on to her, and suddenly raised an arm. For, in the same way she had been with him, she had been with

65

another, and though perhaps this was something he had previously guessed, he had never imagined it clearly, the way he did now, and, having grabbed her by the shoulders, he came down upon her.

But Christine was upright again, they fought each other off for a while. She fell to her knees. She let out a terrible scream. The child too had woken. Jean-Luc said:

—Ask for forgiveness!

She had no desire to; three times she got back on her feet, three times he folded her back down to the ground, and her knees clapped against the floor, she closed her eyes, and he, raising his voice:

—Ask for forgiveness!

Did she hope this forgiveness would come? or was she defeated? At once she slumped forward, her braids hanging before her face; she said:

—Forgive me!

He immediately released her. Having gone to get her clothes from the chair, he brought them to her:

—Dress yourself! he said.

Then returned to the crying child and, taking him in his arms, standing near the bed, rocked him.

At the other end of the bedroom, she had started to put her clothes back on. Slowly she put on her skirt, fastened her waist and her camisole, and, in front of the little mirror, having turned around, did up her chignon again. And, in the mirror, she saw herself, with her blazing eyes and the red blotches on her cheeks; she did up her chignon again, added in the bronze combs; as for him, he remained near the bed, without moving.

When she was finished:

—Are you ready?

She nodded.

—What about your shoes?

She said:

—They're in the kitchen.

—Well then! he said. Come with me!

The little one went on crying, he put him back to bed, he made her pass by him. And, in the kitchen, he said to her:

—Now you can put your shoes back on.

Sitting on the bench, she put her shoes back on, and he continued:

—You can also take your scarf, what's yours is yours.

Obedient, she took her scarf. And, once again, he asked her:

—Are you ready?

And, once again, she nodded.

He went to stand in front of the big door with its heavy lock of wrought iron, which was fixed on the inside by thick crossties; then, sliding the bolt with its beaten handle and small engraved images, the big door opened, he held it open. The night was dark and cold, the wind blowing even harder, with a nasty draft, and the weight of the fog still on the pond; she felt fear in the face of this night. She said:

—Jean-Luc!

He answered:

—Be off!

She bowed her head, she left. At once, he shut the door. In slamming, the latch made a great sound in the silence. He listened, he heard something like a sigh: and for a while she remained on the stoop without moving; then she went down a step, halted again; went down another, and hesitated in this way down the entire staircase. All of a sudden, she burst into laughter, she ran back up the stairs, she knocked at the door with her fist:

—Since I've got one, she screamed, what do I care? What do I care? You've got yours, I've got mine.

She laughed some more, then he heard her walk off. He returned to bed, he had grabbed the child, he was lifting him into his arms. And the little one called:

—Maman! Maman!

He said to him:

—You no longer have a mother.

CHAPTER VI

SHE DID NOT RETURN. IT WAS said that she had gone to live with her sister, where she was to give birth.

And so, not long afterward, Jean-Luc, one morning, left the house. Tall and slightly stooping, they saw him come, after locking his door; he walked slowly, leaning with one hand on a big baton, holding the little one in the other.

First he went to the blacksmith's. The blacksmith was so surprised at how much he had aged that he halted his iron. Jean-Luc said to him:

—She's betrayed me a second time, don't ever mention her to me again!

Meanwhile Marie, having heard him, had come down; he repeated to her:

—Don't ever mention her to me again.

He added:

—I've come to let you know.

He left, he continued on his way, he went off to the village. From time to time, he stopped, sitting on the edge of a wall, a heap of beams, a fence. And everyone thought the same as the blacksmith: "How thin and aged he looks!"

For the little one's sake, he also went to see his two cousins, Théodule and Dominique, then he started back, walking down the little street, passing by the fountain, then along the gardens in front of the houses, which are so small, but square and tidy between the crooked fences. Some women, some girls came; one of them carried a little pot of cream, and walked with precaution; another, light in color, had blond hair and a blue and white apron; some men said hello to Jean-Luc: he continued on his way without answering them.

Great sunlight had spread through the sky again, clearer and brighter, as can sometimes be the case after days of bad weather; the remains of the snow melted, and the edges of the roofs in the shade, still garnished, dripped: then, in the hollow earth, a straight line appears where little stones, unveiled, gleam.

He went home, boiled some water, began to wash the cups and dishes. He swept the kitchen; when it was in order, around midday, he made the soup; he gave it to the little one to eat, clumsily holding out the big spoon to him.

Then placed his hands before him, and told himself: "They're too heavy. Hers were small and light; but her hands have known evil." He went on: "These here, these are mine." He looked up: "We'll put them to use."

Upon which, Félicie having arrived, he put together

a big pile of Christine's clothes, which he gave to her; and he said:

—Take these and bring them to your house. And be off, I don't want to see you anymore!

But she returned, and he took pity on her simple-mindedness; she regained her place by the fire. And thus he entered his new life.

It was difficult, but he held on nevertheless. Others helped him, for they thought: "It's Christine who's in the wrong, not him; he has a lot of qualities; but he doesn't see clearly." Which is why Marie, from the very first day, said to him:

—Jean-Luc, when you leave, be sure to bring me the child, I'll keep him with my own, one more will go unnoticed.

Jéromette too had come. She was a little old woman, who had once had two daughters and one son—and all her children were dead, her husband too, like her children; so she had put her love in flowers to such an extent that they were everywhere in her bedroom, and her windows were garnished with them, as well as her little garden. She said to Jean-Luc:

—I'll watch over the little one too.

So that when he went to the woods, upon his return he found the child well-bathed and well-dressed, which encouraged him to go on living. He made an effort, he said: "I have to show everyone I'm strong!", and lifted his heavy fists. And encouraged himself, grabbing his ax or the wedge for the tree trunks, and when he fell back down, as sometimes happened, he cried: "Get up!", he got back up, for he thought: "I've got this child and he's mine; I have to last for him."

He still found comfort in this, and by repeating it to himself, went on:

"One shouldn't ask for too much." And, sometimes, in the evening, he felt something like relief, the days having come one after the other, like fresh water over a wound; with little pleasures that reappear: to feel his work was accomplished, eating one's fill, smoking before the fire, and heat ran through him, the kind that makes the blood run and the heart beat more at its ease; he went to see the little one who slept, he returned; he told himself: "There, I'm at peace, I've come to terms with it."

Whereas those first days, he constantly searched for Christine, and everything was like an image of her; such was a die he found, a planted nail, the sound of footsteps, or a voice outside, and he turned toward the door, and it was only Félicie, or whoever, just someone passing by. And he felt something break within him, every time. A great weariness also, for he fought it with all of his might, having promised himself never to think of her again. Humiliation each time too, for he told himself: "She's the stronger one!", and he thought: "Is there someone in the world who's unhappier than I am?"

Now he was cured, at least he wanted to believe it and forced himself to. One day the sun came out from behind the forest branches, from where the snow had come down (there were heaps of it at the base of the trees); he saw the sun hoist itself into the air, fling itself at the sky—and, after the intense cold and the sad mornings of winter, it was a great joy to behold. Jean-Luc went to see his fences, they were deteriorating, he told himself: "As soon as the weather's good, I'll begin to rebuild them; the property has to be in good shape for the little one." He also examined the house, which had been neglected during summer, when the days are devoured by work in the fields, and the previous winter too, for he hadn't been around (something he thought long about)—he saw the loose steps on the staircase, the walls dented and cracked; he told himself: "We've lived in disarray, that's all over now!"

He had a little money in a box, which he had saved with difficulty and patience, he counted it, he thought: "I need to double that by next year." And, daydreaming of how he could achieve this: "Well, there isn't much to do this time of year . . . what if I went to see Comby, he needs a worker, and I'm qualified." He went to see Comby, the carpenter; he was hired in no time, he went back to the shooting board, to the gouge, and to the brace.

"For," as he repeated, "land is the best investment, it stays put, it lasts; money just has a pretty sound." Only a sad feeling and grave air remained with him, a certain wisdom had come. When, once again, everything was destroyed in one swoop.

Mardi Gras had arrived, and, because it was beautiful and hot out, he had gone to see the masks, the buffoons, as they're called, and all those who were in the village had done the same, so that, all up and down the street, the benches were filled with people. There were a dozen of these masks; the pack walked up the street, then came back down it.

And so, the elderly, a little removed from life, looked on without saying anything, leaning forward on their hard knees, while the young enjoyed themselves.

The pack walked by, walked by again; with, as is custom, boys dressed as girls—and they all had their faces hidden or else colored with soot, having faked bellies with pillows, having changed their gait, having changed their voices. The game, for those watching, was to try and recognize them; you wondered: "Who's that?" And you figured it out, and you laughed.

They laughed hardest about a buffoon who had just arrived, short and paunchy, walking with a bag full of ashes he threw at girls' faces, and you could hear the girls scream among the laughs, while the paunchy buffoon ran after them. Everyone said: "It has to be Anthime." He was Jean-Luc's neighbor, and had quarreled with him over a share of water; all of a sudden, seeing Jean-Luc, he approached him, and, standing there, legs wide, began to say, pointing to the little one:

—Where'd you find this one here?

The little one, who was afraid, hid behind his father's shoulder. The buffoon went on:

—Was he expensive?

The crowd watched Jean-Luc grow pale. He didn't answer him, except to say:

—Be on your way.

But, as soon as he left, Jean-Luc rose and went home.

That same evening, he had been invited to the blacksmith's, he didn't come; sometime past eight o'clock, someone decided to fetch him; they found the house shut and came back, saying: "He was already asleep."

He was not asleep, quite the opposite, for the thought had entered his head like a worm pierces through wood, he was tormented by it, to the point that all thought of sleep had deserted him. He told himself: "If that was Anthime, he's my enemy, he may have lied; but she too may have lied, she's never done anything but!" Holding the lamp above the child, he went on: "His hair is blond, not black like mine, and, she too, she too had black hair; he's blond like him, ah! my God!" He went to stand before the small mirror, he examined himself. Because the light came from above, his face appeared even more thin and hollow, with two holes instead of eyes, two holes in the middle of his cheeks, creases in his forehead, and his pallor. He thought to himself: "Does he look like me? How can I be sure? What should I do?"

He let himself fall at the end of the bench. Then, much like when a ray of sunshine, on a sad November evening, suddenly pierces through the clouds with a false light, he saw more clearly the misery that was his life. He said: "I can't go on! I can't go on!"

Some girls could be heard laughing on their way home; then came the sound of harmonicas with their light jittery notes, because this was the day of celebration before Lent comes.

The following day, Jean-Luc began to drink. They had to carry him home and put him to bed; they even had a lot of trouble finding the key, which he had hidden in a new place; and old Jéromette, having brought the little one home around six o'clock and finding no one, had to bring him back to hers and put him to bed there.

Jean-Luc fell from bed in the night, woke in the morning on the floor with a bump on his head. He got dressed, went out drinking again. Three days in a row, he drank.

The fourth day, Jéromette returned, still with the child; she said to Jean-Luc:

—I have to keep an eye out to see when you're home. This is ugly behavior, Jean-Luc.

He looked at her without answering, but, when she handed him the little one, whom, despite her old age, she had carried all the way there, he pushed her back hard.

—Lead him, he said, to those who made him.

And so, full of pity, she brought him home again, and now the little one asked for his father, and he cried the entire way back, so that people came out of their houses, and asked:

—What's going on?

—Ah! well, she said, I just don't know what to do anymore.

For she was poor and not strong enough to take care of a child all on her own.

But, a moment later, Jean-Luc also left, walked all the way to see Firmin Craux, who was an old man, rich and very greedy, living at the entrance of the village. In the past he had wanted one of Jean-Luc's cows. Jean-Luc, having entered, offered it to him. Craux asked:

—How much?

—Three hundred, said Jean-Luc.

The old man said:

—That's too much.

For he knew everything. So Jean-Luc began to tell him:

—Listen, I don't need it anymore. Do you like it?

—Yes and no, said Craux.

—Well then! name your price!

Craux told him:

—Two hundred.

It was about half of what Foumette was worth. For she produced eight liters of milk. Even so, Jean-Luc told him:

—Agreed!

But Craux went on:

—One more thing, I'll give you a hundred now and the other hundred in three months; I'll write something up for you.

—Never mind then!

—Alright, then a hundred and seventy up front and you'll bring me the beast at once.

Jean-Luc walked back through the village. It was mild out, the roofs puffed out a vapor. He went to the stable, untied Foumette; he pulled her with the rope, but she mooed, already missing her warm litter, while people said to him:

—What are you doing? Where are you leading her?

But he did not give them an answer. He halted in front of Craux's house. He returned once more, gripping his heavy wallet tight in his pocket. That night, he went out drinking again.

He placed two fifty-franc coins on the table; he said:

—This one's on me.

CHAPTER VII

THE AIR WAS THICK, BLUE AROUND the lamp that hung from the ceiling; they were about seven or eight men, cramped around a table, Jean-Luc in the middle. He had ordered a first liter, which was now finished; he ordered a second, which was soon emptied too; then he cried: "Another one!", which they brought. And he lifted it up while he took out his purse, which he held in the other hand; he went on: "This is still heavier."

—It's because I'm rich! he continued.

And suddenly emptied his purse on the table. The crowns began to roll, the others caught them as they went by, laying them flat before them; they counted them, saying: "Where'd you get all this money from?", and looked at Jean-Luc with fear and respect.

—That's a secret! answered Jean-Luc.

He spoke loudly, in a confident voice; he rummaged through his pocket, he took out two bank bills.

—What about these? he said, laughing.

And he cried:

—Another liter!

But suddenly, they all started to laugh, the cobbler having entered. His name was Nanche, he was a very small man, bald, with a black face and black hands, and a green apron; he only worked about two days a week; the rest of the time, he tended to his thirst, as he said, and added: "It's the leather that dries me up."

He'd gone to sit alone in a corner, they called to him:

—Hey! Nanche, you sulking?

He didn't move, still sober. But because Jean-Luc had started to make his crowns resound again, Nanche began to turn his head from time to time, taking a sideways glance at the shiny money, and shrugged his shoulders.

Upon which, it was Jean-Luc's turn to call him:

—Come on, Nanche! we miss you.

Nanche didn't respond at first; then, when he finished his bottle of eau-de-vie, he suddenly stood up and came over. His eyes shone under his big drooping eyebrows, while he dried his hands on his apron. He said:

—Hello, gang!

—Hurray for us! cried Jean-Luc.

He made him take a seat near him and at once made him drink.

—Here's to you, he started again; when one is happy one drinks well, when one drinks well one is happy.

The noise went on increasing, as well as the smoke; they could barely see one another in the small room, with its great beams that seemed to weigh down on their heads, they spoke of anything, in any which way—the men leaning on their elbows all along the table, their heads down, looking out the corners of their eyes, and they ran their hands over their mustaches; within the group, Nanche, smaller than everyone, and Jean-Luc, pale, who laughed.

And, making him drink once more, he patted Nanche on the back:

—Now you're going to sing us something.

Which is what everyone was waiting for, because that's how it went: when he was drunk, they did with him what they liked, they went so far as to hang him by the thumbs, as once happened, smudging his face, blackening it with tar—all this just to anger him, because that's when the fun began.

—You're going to sing us something! said Jean-Luc.

Nanche stood on the bench, he coughed two or three times, like he always did. He began:

You've got your blonde, I've got my brunette,
I wouldn't want it any other way . . .

It was always the same song, one they all knew well; and Jean-Luc took up the refrain, which all the others burst into after him:

I prefer my brunette, ô gué,
I prefer my bru-u-nette

—Is that right? said Jean-Luc, looking up.

He added:

—Maybe so.

And, during the following refrain, he sang even louder. At that moment, someone pulled the bench; Nanche fell flat on his back. They laughed up a storm. He stood up quickly and cried, clenching his fists:

—Don't touch me! Don't touch me!

But already Jean-Luc had sat him back down:

—You're wasting your time, you're better off drinking.

So Nanche drank some more, and Jean-Luc laughed, saying:

—It's because we're joyous and happy, I tell you, and have jolly hearts, and are filled with trust.

To which the others responded:

—Of course!

But, once again, in response to a sign some-one made, Nanche was surrounded, taken, squeezed, snatched, hoisted to the ceiling, banged up there two or three times against the beams, then abruptly released; and found himself sprawled on the floor, where he remained a moment, stunned. Then, coming back to his senses, he threw himself at those who were there, without know-ing who they were, head down. At first no one could see a thing anymore, for there was great disorder; finally, the door opened, Nanche reappeared, was shoved outside— and, slipping on the stairs, he rolled through the mud;

upon which, the door was shut again. Everyone cried and coughed with laughter.

And Nanche shouted from outside:

—Thieves! Assassins!

While Jean-Luc started up again:

—It's because we've got light jolly hearts.

But soon everything hushed; the square was now empty.

—You'll see, someone said, he'll come back with his leather knife.

Upon which, they all went back to the window. Indeed, Nanche returned, head bare, walking with difficulty, his clothes muddy; and he went to sit on the linden tree's bench, sharpening his blade with a stone; he spoke the whole time, but no one could understand what he was saying. And tall Laurent, opening the window, shouted:

—Hey! Nanche, let's talk it out over here!

He came over, shaking with fury, lifting his iron; suddenly his head went through the open window, with one arm forward, and the lamplight flashed on the leather knife; then the door, which was locked, was shaken, and the wood sounded beneath his kicks; following which, there was a silence, they heard something like sobbing.

—There you go, said tall Laurent, now he's crying.

And so, at the table, where they'd all gone to sit back down, great laughs resounded once more. Except that Jean-Luc no longer laughed; he had pushed his glass back and placed both elbows on the table, his head in his hands. They said to him:

—Hey! Jean-Luc! What's up? You're not drinking anymore.

He shook his head, then, throwing down a coin he took out, he asked: "What does it matter?", paid, took his change, and headed for the door. They cried to him:

—Be careful!

But he didn't listen.

Nanche was sitting on the front steps. Jean-Luc approached him, nudged him with his elbow and said:

—Listen, I was wrong, because you and I are brothers.

Then he held out his hand to him. The cobbler looked up, and in the window's gleam, they stared into each other's faces. And Nanche said:

—Come with me.

Jean-Luc followed him. It rained from a low sky weighing down on roofs; the sky barely prevailed, due to a crescent moon being lost behind clouds, a lack of clarity in the air, inside which the houses were square and black. They walked together, linking arms. And when they were at Nanche's house, at the other end of the square, he went on:

—You have to come in.

And so Jean-Luc did, and he repeated:

—You and I are brothers.

—Is that true? said Nanche, who was now sitting down. They've taken my honor.

Jean-Luc responded:

—Mine too, they've taken my honor too.

Nanche had his bed in what looked like the kitchen, a straw mattress laid out on the floor; one of the table's legs was missing, this leg had been replaced by an upright crate; on the hearth, near the marmite of polenta, there was a pot of pea fondue; spiderwebs hung all about.

They became friends, Nanche having said:

—You're right.

They sat side by side before the hearth. They'd blown on the ash, where there remained a few embers that sizzled back to life, and the bundle of sticks blazed. Jean-Luc said:

—Are you here for me? Maybe you are, you see, because we were six children, and three are dead, and of the other three, two are far away, and my father is dead too and I chased off my wife, and as for the child, they say he isn't mine.

Nanche repeated:

—So it's true that we're brothers?

He shook his head:

—It's like Our Lord, they shared his robe among themselves, they beat him, whipped him, they spat in his face, they put him on.

And in the light of the bright flame, which trembled on the walls:

—Well, they beat me, knocked me down, and they say: "He's crying." I answer them: "What are eyes for?"

But Jean-Luc shouted in a terrible voice:

—And they kneel before money! Look, look what I do with it!

He had taken the bills from his pocket, held them out to the flame. It bit into their corners, spread rapidly; and, the paper having slipped from his fingers, it fell into the cinders. Only a bit of white ash remained, which Jean-Luc crushed with his feet. Nanche hadn't moved an inch. He only said:

—It's really burning up!

Then they remained without speaking, still very close. The stillness of night encircled the house. And Jean-Luc felt his rage die down, and, the wine haze having dispersed through his head, what he needed now was to rest and have someone near him, and he thought: "I've got someone here," thinking of Nanche—but, having turned around, he realized that Nanche had fallen asleep. He slept, his head against Jean-Luc's shoulder. And Jean-Luc, pulling out the straw mattress, laid him out on it.

And so, once again, he found himself completely alone with himself. And once again he was no longer sure of anything. Yet, when Nanche writhed in his dreams, crying: "Leave me alone!", suddenly sitting up, waving his arms—each time Jean-Luc went to him and put him back to bed. Then, in the end, he yielded to sleep; he lay down at Nanche's side. He slept until morning.

When he came home, his back was white, and spiderwebs were caught at the brim of his hat. He walked along the houses, with his red eyes, a fire in his head. He told people: "The most evil ones aren't always the ones you think."

—You say: I drink. Well yes, I drink! But is there a sparkle in my glass? They've got a hard heart, you see.

When he got home, he heard the blacksmith calling to him:

—Hey! Jean-Luc, he said, it can't go on like this, your little one spent the night at ours, and my wife already has four children to take care of.

For a moment, he hesitated, then he responded:

—Leave me alone!

—Don't listen to what people say! continued the blacksmith.

But Jean-Luc shook his head and, without adding anything, closed the door behind him.

That afternoon, he drank again; this time he went to sit alone in a corner with Nanche; he said: "We understand each other." Nanche had something like respect for him; they stayed together all evening. And, when tall Laurent approached to start the teasing again, Jean-Luc looked him straight in the eye and said:

—Don't touch him anymore, you understand, I'm here now!

He no longer left the inn, he was never at home anymore. So that he was not there to receive his mother the day she came, a week later. Hearing the rumors regarding her son, the money thrown afar, his passion for drinking, and, besides, even more self-interested than proud, she had thought: "I must go." She found Félicie in the kitchen with the little one; and the poor thing did not grasp who she was, nor did she have the concerns of orderly women, for that requires reason: the bed wasn't made, the clothes were scattered across the room; there was a stench and great filthiness; the little one had cried, the tears on his cheeks had crusted into white lines. The old woman said to Félicie: "Be off!" She chased her away. She rolled up her skirt, scrubbed and cleaned until evening.

At that moment, Jean-Luc returned. There came the loud sound of voices, which quickly ceased; then old Philomène came back down the stairs, and she went back through the entire village, having no choice, but without speaking to anyone, nor turning around.

Jean-Luc went on drinking. And another piece of his meadow sold for the little money Craux gave him (who kept an eye on him now); it was one of the best pieces, the one in Roussettes, which he cared about; but he didn't seem to regret the way his property was being dismantled, piece by piece, so disconnected he was from it all. To such an extent that, one day, running into Augustin, when the latter made a detour, he cried to him:

—Take the shortest way, I have no desire to lay a hand on you.

He no longer even had respect for religion, or so it seemed, for he no longer attended mass; the beautiful season now here, the processions had started again, making the rounds of the cemetery; he remained standing behind the wall, watching, and they heard him say: "It's all playacting!"

Yet the new spring was bright and gay, it seemed to rinse the heart, the vines had never been so beautiful, which explained the contentment—along with the crops and the wheat of a good height, and the grass early grown. Even the clouds are pleasant to watch, small and white in the sky, like daisies in the grass; a tall woman passed on the road, with a lamb in her arms.

People greeted one another near the crosses. The bisse men came home from work in packs, with their pickaxes and shovels over their shoulders, they removed their hats when they walked by the cross. They had returned water to the bisse. The streams, all swollen, twirling along the thaw's yellow water, jumped over the bridges one day, then declined and went dry. The toads, on humid nights, ambled down the paths.

Jean-Luc went on drinking. Félicie watched the little one. She sat by the pond under a willow. The bank comes down steeply toward the water, which is immediately deep, and black in its depth; but, at the surface, it glimmers with the blue of the sky, the white of the snow, the green of the meadows; and there are also the reflections of the little trees and the bushes leaning over the water, such as the willow Félicie sat under.

Little Henri played near her, rolling his ball of thread;

or he climbed onto her lap, and having put down her knitting, she'd start to sing.

But other times, too, she seemed to get lost outside of herself in things, with eyes that no longer saw anything, fixed on a point in the immensity before her, her spirit in flight afar; the house was empty over there; the little one, left alone, ran after the grasshoppers.

CHAPTER VIII

ON THAT DAY (IT WAS NEARING the end of May), he found himself, as always, sitting with Nanche at the inn, it was four in the afternoon, it was beautiful and mild out. On the square, in the sun, the linden tree's shadow was already round. In front of the shop was a mule, tied by a rope to a wall, with its wooden packsaddle, where a man put down a great sack of bran, securing it tightly. At that instant, the prior's rooster, out with its chicken, got up on its legs, and began to sing. A great white cloud appeared behind the roofs, and extended toward the top of the sky, like a dog with its paws on the wall.

Jean-Luc pushed back his hat, the cobbler sighed, he pointed to the empty bottle:

—One more?

Jean-Luc shook his head no. They fell back into silence.

At once, from behind Nanche's house, a man appeared, head bare, running; he climbed the front steps, opened the door of the drinking room and shouted:

—Jean-Luc, you need to come now.

—Why's that? said Jean-Luc.

The man repeated:

—Come quickly, I tell you!

And he left in the same way he arrived.

Jean-Luc said:

—They can try to fetch me as much as they'd like, I like it here, I'm staying.

But the cobbler had risen and was looking outside. Then another man came, with a woman, both of them out of breath, and, from outside the inn, they called once again:

—Jean-Luc! Jean-Luc!

Upon which, Nanche opened the window. They went on:

—Tell him to come if he's with you!

And the woman said:

—It's a tragedy! a tragedy!

So Jean-Luc, now also standing, asked:

—What is it?

They answered:

—Come already!

He walked out, took a left; he walked askew, with the man and woman, and the cobbler who followed.

There were a lot of people by the pond, a whole group standing around something on the ground, and everywhere, in the meadows, men and women came running. "My God!" they cried; and, among those who had stopped, someone was lifting both the arms, an old woman had crouched down and held the head in her hands; there were two girls who had approached, and who now ran off; as well as two or three women who were there with their children, and, so as to hide their eyes, covered their faces with their aprons. And the blacksmith, whom they'd gone to fetch, had come, his hammer in hand; now he had thrown his hammer in the grass. Hence, because of all of the people arriving, the group continuously did and undid itself, and the entity moved in the sunshine, with voices you could hear coming, then a silence, then a scream once again—while, behind her willow, Félicie was crouching, and at times she looked quickly to one side, then lowered her head again, placing her hands back over her eyes.

The sun poured onto the gray roofs and the large rocks covering them; on the smooth water of the pond was the fine lace formed by the little drafts of air that dip their fingers there in in jest; and in the little trees, which seemed braided of yellow straw, because of the new leaves, you could see moving and glimmering. But what you could not see, was what was lying on the ground.

The blacksmith had leaned forward with another man, who wore an old hat and had a large beard beneath his eyes. The latter said:

—We have to hang him by the feet.

The blacksmith however:

—What would be the use?

Someone asked:

—Was the poor thing in the water long?

—Quite some time . . . Can't you see! he's as dead as they come.

Someone asked again:

—How did it happen?

—Well, said a woman, I heard Félicie scream, I thought: "That's Félicie screaming, what's going on?" So I went to have a look and I saw some movement in the pond; what?—like a duck flapping its wings; so I screamed too; then Hippolyte came, and he went to fish him out, but it was hard, the others had to come and help him, and yes he was close to the edge, but the water was deep there . . .

—Ah! my God! someone said.

—Hippolyte, lift his head, you see, it falls right back down.

—Look at all that foam!

Some women had started to cry.

—Ah! poor thing! they repeated.

And, when some youngsters arrived, the blacksmith chased them away with kicks, saying:

—Go on, scram, vermin!

Meanwhile, Jean-Luc was on his way. At once they saw him appear from between the houses; he walked with his hands in his pockets, without looking up, with the man and the woman; he was nearing, so they all moved out of his way, and, as if through a door that now opened, what had not been visible came into sight.

And it was little Henri. He was lying on the grass, his robe fully soaked and now void of color; you could see, coming out of it, his skinny legs in blue stockings, with the big shoes and their hooks and brass eyes; his little arms, as if detached from his body, seemed to have been set down beside him. And his head, because of its roundness, seemed very big, the hair stuck to the forehead, from which drops still rolled down onto his purple cheeks every now and again; some weeds in his hair; the eyes had come out of their sockets, like the eyes of someone who was strangled.

Jean-Luc did not speak; he just stared. He must have been thinking: "Who is that?" So great is the distance between what contains life and the same being when deprived of it; he remained motionless for a time; then asked:

—What is it?

No one was speaking, no one was moving either; a breath of air came through once more with its curled outline on the pond, you could hear some movement in the branches; the blacksmith at last:

—Jean-Luc, it's a tragedy!

He looked up at the blacksmith, and, with a changed voice:

—Serves me right, I'm punished!

Then, abruptly, crouching down, he grabbed the child and took him away.

And, at first, because of the body's moisture and cold

temperature, he shivered, and almost hesitated, but only the length of a thought; now, nearly running, he went off in the direction of his house, clutching his child in his arms. And the others, in their astonishment, remained a moment without moving, then all began to follow him, the men and the women, forming a cortege behind him. And, having reached the house, they all went up the stairs and entered the kitchen. But they saw it was empty; there was only, there in the middle, on the newly black tiles, a damp trail.

Marie said:

—He's in the bedroom.

She went to push the latch: the door was locked. She called:

—Jean-Luc, it's me!

No one answered; she listened, you couldn't hear a thing. The kitchen was full, and many people waited outside the house as well; little by little they left, little by little the kitchen also emptied itself, only Marie and two women remained, but, at the hour of supper, they too had to leave.

Félicie, all alone, had not moved from under the willow. The sun went down and touched the tip of the great pointed Bourni, which turned black against the illuminated sky; it crept into the shining ball like a corner, by which the ball was cracked, split from the bottom, then bitten more deeply and halved. Next, like from an ember that collapses, a dust of sparks ascended high in the sky.

From all sides the golden horizon opened up, along with the vastness of the land, with its thousands of mountains, and a vapor ascended from within the cavities, while the pond now descended into shadows little by little, and the round snows of the summits, suspended above things by a succession of forest and rockery, from which the beautiful radiance of day slowly fled, were, on the contrary, flowering and painted with pink. And, farther away, all around the church, you could hear the village stir, with the voices, the cracks of the whip, the clear ringing of the cowbells; but here it was silence that reigned, the house was empty, the kitchen filled with black.

One o'clock sounded at the church tower. Then, the shadows having accumulated, and the snows having extinguished and melted above, the angelus began to ring with the soft sound of its bell, following which the three strokes of the prayer came, fell one by one.

When night came, Marie reappeared, accompanied by her husband; once again she went to knock on the bedroom door:

—Jean-Luc! she said . . .

She went on:

—Let me in, you need help, and you'll have to make a statement.

Then it was the blacksmith who knocked, and he said:

—Don't stay alone, you have to conserve your strength.

Yet, once again, Jean-Luc did not answer.

When the day was over, some people had returned, chatting in a whisper before the house, they said to the blacksmith:

—Well?

He answered them:

—He hasn't moved, he's locked up!

People wondered: "What's he doing? What's the matter with him?" Nobody knew.

Yet, later still, some neighbors having gone to the bell ringer's house, they saw a light in Jean-Luc's bedroom. And, from the bell ringer's house, which is a little higher up, you could see into the bedroom and glimpse one corner of the bed. They saw that Jean-Luc was sitting in front of the bed.

The little one was on the bed; he had been dressed in a new robe; he wore a bonnet of knitted wool, which was tight around his temples and embellished with pink and blue; the crucifix, which had already been of use, was of use once more, lying on his chest; a candle burned on the table, with the cup of holy water and the twig plunged inside it.

And Jean-Luc was by the bed; he was sitting on a chair; he moved little more than the dead.

They went to fetch Marie, who came, her husband too, everyone looked out the window. They asked themselves: "What on earth is he doing?" They thought: "He's been drinking all day, he's under the influence of wine."

And they did not dare to disturb him, in any case they understood it would be pointless. So they said: "Let's wait until tomorrow." And they did.

The night was clear, with a thousand large and white stars that swayed gently through the sky; and soon the croaking of frogs began to travel from one side of the pond to the other.

The following day, early in the morning, Jean-Luc went to the village. He walked upright, did not seem sad, on the contrary he seemed to have recovered some liveliness and vigor. He said to those he met on the road:

—I'm so happy, he's back.

In the afternoon, he went out again, because of the preparations; he began to say:

—I'm sure of it this time, he's really mine.

And, Marie having returned, he allowed her to enter, she put everything in order; his mother had come too, he spoke to her like in the old days.

And so two days passed, and the whole time people came, as is the custom, even though the little body was very ugly and swollen, and the face black: women with their children, men, boys, girls, the door was left open, and they said a prayer with the sign of the cross; it lasted until Friday, which was the day of the burial. The little coffin was easily built with a board sawed into four pieces, it was nailed together, painted blue with a white cross, it was brought over Thursday evening; Friday morning, the little one was lowered inside.

Then they lifted the miserable crate and placed it on two stools before the door, with paper roses as decoration, a white sheet, and, on top of it, a lighted lamp, because the flame indicates that true life does not extinguish. Until morning, a rather strong wind had blown, so that great herds of clouds traversed the sky; they disappeared little by little behind the mountains, and the sun appeared, while the neighbors and two or three close relatives arrived. And the beautiful pink flowers sparkled, with some geraniums borrowed from Jéromette, left in their pots, arranged on the ground around the casket; then, at nine o'clock, the bell started, not the one for men, big and with the muffled toll, but the little one, clear and rung on the fly.

Then, they placed the pole on the little coffin, and fastened it with rope they tightly wound all the way around; a boy grabbed it on each end. Ahead of the coffin went the cross, the one that would be planted on the tomb; behind came Jean-Luc, two or three women, two or three men; they had taken a little street, the sun, still low in the sky, only lit up the top of the roofs; but suddenly the tall pointed church tower appeared, upright in the air, and it sparkled from top to bottom.

The swallows, which had returned, were all through the air; they cried, delighted by the morning, with a flight as sharp as the stroke of the sickle, and along the church wall you could feel the heat of the stones already infused with the sun. But it was humid inside; there, prayers and words of consolation were spoken, and everyone listened, leaning forward or kneeling, while the sunshine, coming in through the great windows, unwound among the benches and onto the tiles like ribbons of color, with the golden objects that glowed on the altar, and the statues of saints and the suspended paintings.

Then, the service was over, they walked out into broad daylight. Just opposite the door is the cemetery gate; it was already open and the tomb was there, in the corner for children. They walked for a moment down the path in the middle. Among the little mica stones and the dry and cracked soil, where the tilting blue crosses pierce through the earth, the good heat had hastened first growths for the carnations and tall irises, which were not yet flowering. The flies circled, awake, the wasps, the bees—the men grabbed the little coffin and lowered it down effortlessly, as light as it was short. When the holy water was thrown, they looked over at Jean-Luc; they saw he was not crying.

Back home, he cried no more than before, calm and rested. Those who were there ate and drank at the kitchen table; speaking of the little one, someone said: "That's it, he's gone now."

A smile crept on Jean-Luc's face, he answered: "Not the real one."

CHAPTER IX

HE CONTINUED: "YOU CAN GO HOME in peace, because he's mine, and the only thing left to me." It was time to leave him. And they all left, his mother too, like he wanted.

Already, that same evening, they became acquainted with his madness, but even more so the following day. For he came to the blacksmith's, and they hadn't seen him there for some time; he sat with everyone on the bench outside the house. It faces the gardens, people often rest there a while, waiting for nightfall, they chat, they tell each other the latest; the blacksmith is in on it all, and skillfully recounts things, making the others laugh.

Between the little fences, there were two or three plum trees; a little farther off, some wooden beehives, painted all sorts of colors and in a straight line; the bees who had returned buzzed inside them, they sounded like a spinning wheel; the branches were full to the brim with birds who went to sleep.

And so Jean-Luc arrived, arms folded like when one carries a child; they thought: "Is it possible?" Yes, he thought he still had his, he carried him like a real child; then, sitting down, he started to rock him; he spoke to him, he told him: "Sleep, little one! Are you comfortable?" He went on: "You no longer have a mother, but you've got your father. Well then! sleep, he's right here." And bounced his knees up and down.

And then, because the others had hushed in their surprise, he asked them: "Why aren't you talking? . . ." They began to speak in order not to upset him, but soon Jean-Luc interrupted them: "More softly, he's fallen asleep." He lowered his own voice.

Two lovers passed behind a barn, they held each other tight, hiding from the gaze of others, so as to be more alone, and tilting under one same weight and one same secret; they came out of the shadows, which they reentered straightaway. And a burning star showed itself on Le Bourni, first lamp in the sky that signals to those beneath, which lit up in their turn. Jean-Luc went on speaking in a whisper; suddenly he rose, saying: "Here comes the cold, I have to put him to bed, he could fall ill."

And he went off.

They said: "Did you see that?" and they understood his behavior the previous days, and his countenance at the burial; that same night the rumor spread through the entire village, where people halted to tell each other the news, and ran all the way to the inn, where the blacksmith purposely came, and repeated: "He's gone mad!" while the cobbler lifted his hat and said: "He's a saint!"

They quickly realized that his was a particular kind of madness, for it had not consumed his entire mind and carried off his reason; he had it there in a corner, if you could put it that way; for the rest, he retained his common sense. And, cheerfulness having returned to him, he went off laughing on the paths, which were now filled with people, as the summer incites going out, and the meadows too were filled with people.

First, they were surprised, then out of habit, no one thought about it anymore. He came and went, carrying his child, they left him to it. Only sometimes, when he passed the washhouse, which was always filled with women scrubbing their boards, one of them, looking up, would cry: "Hey! Jean-Luc, how's your little one?" He would answer: "He's well, thanks." And all of them would start to laugh but, far from turning angry, he would laugh along with them. They went on: "So you like walking now, do you?" And he: "The little one needs air."

Indeed, he no longer did a thing; he left his meadows to the Good Lord's wind, and his grain to the beaks of birds. They had told him: "Lease them at least." He hadn't wanted to. And pointing to the child: "I've neglected him, I've got to redeem myself!"

To go on living, he had sold his second cow. So, when he was not down the paths or in the village, you could find him in front of his house. There, sitting on the bench, his legs wide, with a square of old fabric laid out at his feet for the child that he had, which was an

105

empty place in the eyes of others, he spent his time carving wood into beasts, figurines, women in large skirts, men with pointed hats—all sorts of toys and objects for Henri, as he said, when pointing to them; he held them out to the child; when they fell to the floor: "He doesn't know how to hold them yet!"

And then:

—How do you think he's doing? he looks well.

People didn't know how to answer, they said:

—He looks well.

—And he sure looks like me.

Other times, he spoke of his wife:

—She abandoned me, she went and cheated. But now, adieu!

He also said:

—You see, things change; this wound here (he rolled up his pants), anyone recall where it was anymore?

The violent spring winds had torn the slate off the eaves; the water coming through the holes ran down the front steps; yet the swallows, who liked this spot, had come to it to make their nests, and the mother arrived with worms and insects, while the little ones all held out their wide open beaks to her. At the edge of the pond the bulrush and reeds grew, lifting their pale thin leaves in the air. The cobbler came and said:

—I respect you, you see further than others.

The goats and the heifers were beginning to come out, in the morning the trumpet sounded through the village; and, on Sunday, people went to lie beneath the trees, forming groups that were pretty to see, with the blue and black hats of girls; the sheep bleated along the bank. And so it was that one Sunday, Théodule, on his way back from visiting a wheat field with his wife, passed by the pond, and saw Jean-Luc exit his house with a ladder, go to his apple tree, a little one flowering just then, place his ladder there, and, climbing to the top of the tree, begin to pick the flowers.

Théodule, approaching him, cried:

—What are you doing?

—It's a bouquet for the little one.

He went on picking, tearing out entire branches, with the little tree that was becoming bare and black little by little, while Théodule's wife said: "My God! is it possible? All of this gone, all of this wasted!" Upon which Théodule continued:

—Leave him the fruits instead.

But Jean-Luc shook his head. "He asked me," he said. Because now he imagined that the little one spoke to him. He descended from the tree with a big bouquet, as many flowers as he could carry.

It was still another matter altogether the day of the Corpus Christi procession, which is one of the great celebrations. On that day the procession loops through the entire village; and along the streets, everywhere it had to pass, acacias had been planted, all powdered of fine white snowflakes, and cut from the hedges. In addition, three great altars had been erected and decorated with images and vases, with garlands full of daisies. Then, to the sound of the bells, when the hour had come, the entire village set off for church, from where the procession left. Long as could be, with the crosses, the colored banners, the soldiers and their beautiful uniforms, the fanfare, the drums, the little girls and their white chiffon dresses, crowns in their hair, the girls beneath their veils, and the men and the women, walking in two rows and singing, it uncoiled through the village to the altar near the fountain, returned, went around again; the bells were ringing, the mortars left.

Jean-Luc went home directly after Mass and reappeared wearing an old helmet from the time of the Pope's Guards, which he had found in the attic, all spotted with rust, the panache eaten by worms. As for the rest, he had kept his ordinary clothes on; dressed in this way, he followed the procession. When people looked surprised, he told them: "It's to please the little one. He laughed so hard when he saw me."

Even so, he sang as much as possible, pious once more, and prayed with fervor. Then, the procession over, people began to celebrate; there was a dinner at city hall, with a ball afterward, in which men dance among themselves, to the drum; he danced with the bell ringer, he danced with Théodule.

The beautiful summer had arrived, shining at windows in bright flames; the vapors take pleasure in this.

Sometimes, when the evening returned cool temperatures, he went off to Le Chemin de Finges, which races flat against the slope, bordered with briars and bushes and their white clusters. He walked there, carrying the child, and spoke to him.

Girls arrived in packs, because it's the season for socializing, and the heart is like flowers, which have a window for blooming. They came holding hands. As they advanced, troops of little birds, bursting into the air from branches, flew along the hedge, landing farther, then shooting back into the air; people hollered from every direction. The girls would halt to respond and the cries came and went, the call from afar and the clear response; then they got going again, the evening air ruffling their aprons.

He sat down, awaiting them.

—And the suitors?

—Lost on the way!

He took the child (whom they could not see):

—Would you like one to replace them?

—Sure, if he's of age.

And Sidonie said:

—Does he like brunettes or blondes?

They stood before him; they laughed, looked down, in their gray and blue dresses with the small velvet stripes.

—Well, said Jean-Luc, he's blond, so he likes brunettes best.

He continued: "Isn't that right, little one? . . . He

says yes . . . You see he was too blond before, now he's golden . . . He's not for you, Sidonie."

She was blonde too, as she well knew, having looked at herself in the mirror; she was proud of her blond mane. Then, showing her teeth, with her clear beautiful laugh:

—And you, what do you like best?

—Oh! me? he asked, I'm too old for that . . . he's replaced me.

And he held out his empty arms to them, and they were not surprised, aware of his peculiarity, yet moved back, a little embarrassed, while he continued:

—You're all being rather difficult!

Jean-Luc and the pack of girls headed back together, and from within thicker shadows, the pond gleamed like a silver dish. They chatted, passing by the painter's house; a little yellow dog barked, and, at the windows, there were crates painted blue and filled with geraniums. Then Jean-Luc continued alone, having said goodnight to the girls.

He had become very handsome, with his long beard, which was black and curly, and his hair was black and curly. He was paler and as if taller, with a dash of steady fire in his dark eyes gazing out in the distance, the taut skin of his forehead, and pronounced eyebrows.

Recognizable at once, because of his height and the way he walked, legs bent, his upper body leaning forward; in his black Sunday clothes, which he wore all week, a black bow at his tie, a black felt hat.

Again he had sold one of his meadows to Firmin Craux, and it was said that his mother was trying to impose a ban on him.

And yet others nearly envied him, though his happiness was false; but not to him, who was firm in his folly, in such a way that he did not suffer at all. People were surprised by the gentleness of his voice.

The month of August came. The old Ambroise, Christine's father, died.

CHAPTER X

HE WAS ROTTEN ON THE INSIDE, like a tree trunk eaten by worms, hanging on only by the bark; and were a gust of wind to come, it would break. One more time they saw him go all the way to the fountain, limping and hunched over with age, wearing his faded blue garment; and a while later return, he who coughed and spat, and halted at each step; he died in the night, he made no sound in dying: at daybreak they found him in the door opening, between the bedroom and the kitchen, fallen to the ground, fully dressed; his mouth was open, having died of suffocation; the neighbor said to Félicie: "What's wrong with your father?" she didn't know; they touched him, he was already cold. So, the death knell having started to toll, people halted on paths, people said: "Who is it?" "It's Ambroise." "Well," they said, "he's done his time." And the following day Christine came back up, with her child, the new one, to whom she'd just given birth.

That same night, the blacksmith, having run into Jean-Luc, was so shocked by his countenance, that he remained standing there, watching him. Jean-Luc went off with his hands in his pockets, suddenly halted and lifted an arm; then turning around to face the blacksmith:

—You haven't seen him? he cried.

—Who's that?

—The little one.

—No, said the blacksmith.

And Jean-Luc (alerted of Christine's return):

—My God! he continued, he was afraid of her, he left.

And sat on a wall with his head in his hands.

The next day, old Ambroise was lowered into the ground. They left him his blue garment, for it no longer served a purpose. And Christine remained in the village, having inherited her father's property. She lay with her child on the old man's bed; the dip in the mattress was still there. But from that day on she didn't leave the house without first checking that Jean-Luc wasn't out in the neighborhood; and she avoided him thus.

He was always on the road however, feverish with movement and walking; never still, never in one place, he spoke, he said: "He got the hell out of here, I've got to look for him . . . He went off, because of her. He was afraid, you see, she's been a bad mother; he told me she wanted to poison him; and he left, end of story!" He went on: "And so I'm looking for him."

—And I told myself: "Perhaps he's only hiding." So I went and looked in the upstairs bedroom, I moved everything, searched everything, I checked all through the kitchen, along with the cave and the hayloft, nothing! nothing! and went to the pond, went all the way around it, there are bushes, I looked inside of them, and then went through the village, have you seen him? tell me the truth . . . Ah! it's a tragedy!

He went from house to house, shaking his head. He continued: "You see, I can't live without him anymore, I've got a void here, a void in my head." He left with his same great strides.

Then for about two or three days, no one saw him anymore, he had gone to look in the woods. Around Le Bourni, where the bisse pulls away as a tunnel, there are precipices; he ran alongside the bisse, in his turmoil. They said to him: "Could a child make it through there? We can only barely make it through." He answered: "You see, he's not like the others."

He went up to the mayens, where people came to live on two different occasions during the year, now empty, his own empty too; from there he went off to the high prairie, already rocky, came back down; he went all the way around the ponds again, entering the remote hay-lofts, where there's hay, where one can sleep; he returned in the evening, his beard gray with dust, his shirt on his arm; he let himself collapse with weariness on the bench outside the house, and did not think to start a fire, to make himself something to eat.

At times Marie brought him a bowl of soup. And, more formal with him now:

—Is it reasonable, may I ask, to live like a true savage?

She showed him the holes in the roof, the loose stairs: "You won't make it if you go on like this."

He answered:

—I don't care, I need him back.

The swallows had gone to bed, having long circled the house with their little evening cries; it was as if a garment of silence had been placed over things, and over there, the little skinned apple tree, naked and black, with its leafless branches. He went on:

—I need to go to bed, and wake up early. Tomorrow I'll go to La Bouille.

But, an idea having come to him, the following Sunday, directly after midday, he went down to the bottom, to his mother's. The weather was typical of summer, bright and beautiful, even stormy, with heavy clouds resting on the flat mountaintops, and the flies stung more strongly. It's the season of thick shadows, and the gray leaves that stick together hang in clumps from the weakened branches, while rods of sunshine are planted upright in the earth. He had gone by way of the valley path, done and redone time and time again: there, among the rolling stones, along the stream and round bushes, walk, on a daily basis, the men and the mules, the women knitting their stockings, the youngsters returning from school; he came down in hurried strides. Soon the path veers a little; with pinewoods you enter, and at first the terrain is flat, then the slope picks back up, and the roots,

116

jutting out, twist upon it like snakes. There is a fountain, another bend, then the path sinks straight to the bottom; and you come upon La Pierre des Morts, which is a great flat stone that seems deliberately placed at the edge of the path, having acquired its name because of the coffins that are brought up to the parish cemetery, placed on the stone just long enough for the transporters to catch their breath. Then, slightly beneath the stone, the woods cease, and the orchards begin.

Among the new grass flowed the fresh water, with its beautiful hues, which combined to make green; taking advantage of the sun, and also because of the first ripe grapes, many had come down; the whole bottom was filled with people, even though it was the season where it still remained uninhabited. At a bend in the road, two or three couples twirled to the tune of harmonicas; farther down, between the apple trees, which, seen from above, were like balls, completely round and without trunks, boys and girls were sitting or lying down, or else ran, chasing each other. Then came the vines that collapse through the prairie in great distressed banks, between little walls and strange rocky tips; stony, all of it, and shining in the sun, with, finally, the back of the valley and the river, straight and white like a road.

From there, some steam rose; along the river, a train left, dragging on like a black worm; and, on the pointed summits of the opposite mountains, which were already faintly engulfed in the blue, some clouds, new and white, not belonging to the ones still in place, had been caught, and, as if held by a string, dangled, then tore off, carried elsewhere by the sky's highest winds, while weight and tranquility reigned below.

And Jean-Luc went off to the left, toward his mother's house, along with two or three other structures, for this entire zone of the mountain was made up of such hamlets. White houses of stone, decrepit under their flat roofs; sundials with numbers painted blue. You could hear the sound of the drums, in an orchard the fanfare played.

He paid attention to nothing. He asked the first person he encountered:

—Have you seen my mother?

—She was here a moment ago.

He entered, did not find her, and, walking outside, did not find her where she sometimes came to sit in front of the house, being of an age that requires heat; a vine hung from some trellises, it allowed for a little shade. Meanwhile, in front of a cellar belonging to Baptiste the hunter, some men drank, and two dogs were lying at the foot of a small almond tree. Just then, Baptiste lifted his glass, saying: "One more week and we can take out the shotguns." Seeing Jean-Luc, he cried to him:

—Hey! have you come for a drink?

But Jean-Luc shook his head, he repeated: "Have you seen my mother?" They answered him: "She just left, come have a drink while you wait for her, we'd like your company, we never see you anymore." He lifted a hand: "Those days are over!" He entered the kitchen.

After some time, his mother arrived; he walked right up to her, she didn't have time to speak:

—Is he here? he asked her.

She had small gray eyes, deep-set, with a hat pulled over them, and hands like the knots in vines. And she watched him with those little eyes, she forced them upon him:

—Come in, she said, if you have something to say to me.

And she pushed him inside. "Is he here?" "You've got something to say? Well have a seat,—I do too." She had pulled out the bench for him.

—Ah! he said, I see, you don't have him either, and yet I've searched for him everywhere.

Meanwhile she had gone to fetch a piece of bread and a quarter of cheese from the cupboard beneath the hayrack, she set them down before Jean-Luc with a full bottle of wine, she said to him:

—Eat and drink, then you'll head back up.

But he interrogated her, saying:

—Why won't you answer me?

—Ah! poor soul, she said. What have you done with your property? You made a fool of me with your marriage, you said: "Go to hell!" She made a cuckold of you, you returned, I took you back, you left again. And now, what sort of life do you live? ah, and whose son are you?

They say you're mine, ha! I no longer believe it; when I look at you I think: "Is that my son?" I'll say it again; eat and drink, and then you'll head back up, for I don't know you anymore.

He was quiet, neither ate nor drank; when she was done speaking, he only said:

—Will you answer me?

He continued:

—Because if you're telling the truth, I have to head back.

But she, approaching him:

—Is it your child you're looking for? And yet you're well aware he's dead.

He looked up, and began to laugh.

—Who told you that?

—I saw it with my own two eyes.

—You must be blind; listen to me, I'm the one who sees clearly.

And, with the tips of his fingers, he touched his eyes. She remained her mouth open with surprise. The sky was now overcast and some clouds lay across the sun, so that the light had dropped abruptly: the kitchen was in total darkness. Jean-Luc continued:

—I've got ears, I've got eyes and ears.

In front of the house, Baptiste and the others chatted outside of the cellar; the fanfare no longer played. And the wind, high in the sky, came from the eastern side, which was made visible by a purple hue, high above

120

the mountain, which was growing with haste; the grass tilted, the vine shoot leaves trembled. Then the little cat entered the kitchen. But the old woman approached him again:

—They were right!

And he: "Who?" "Those who say you're crazy!"

He lifted his baton, he banged on the table.

"Yes," she was saying, "you're crazy!" He banged harder on the table, he was screaming: "If you've got him, give him back, and if you've hidden him, come clean!" And each time he lifted his baton. So she began to call: "Baptiste, come, he's breaking everything!"

Upon which Baptiste arrived; and, from all the neighboring houses, people, drawn by the noise, had come running and asked: "What is it?" But Jean-Luc, seeing Baptiste enter, moved back to the bedroom door; he was saying: "Don't touch me! don't touch me! because otherwise . . .", and again he lifted his baton. The old woman kept repeating: "If you hadn't come, he would've broken everything!"

The wind rose, it whistled through the chimney.

Baptiste said:

—What do you want?

And Jean-Luc:

—I want the little one.

They looked at one another, they shrugged their shoulders. Someone said: "Let's throw him out." But Baptiste, raising his voice:

—You've made enough noise as it is, you hear; stay calm, or we'll tie you up.

He said to Mathieu:

—Go and fetch a rope.

Just then the storm was bursting. The great sound of thunder roared, and, at the same time, a mass of water resembling a wave came crashing down on the front steps, splashing into the kitchen. They could still hear Jean-Luc saying to his mother: "You promise you don't have him?" She answered: "I promise." He walked out.

A gust of wind took hold of him, and he spun in it with his hat, which had flown off and fell back into the puddles that had already formed, and the stream of the furrowed banks; he ran after it and slipped; the people who had taken refuge under the eaves burst into laughter. Someone cried to him: "You should've worn your helmet!" Upon which, the laughter increased, while he moved away, climbing straight up the slope.

He climbed, holding on with both hands to the bushes, among the thick mud that ran, where his shoes remained caught, despite the aridity of the ground, which was poorly dressed in patches of grass; then higher up among the scrub and rough little trees; then through a wheat field, some meadows; and the sleeves of his shirt were glued to his arms, while the water, having pierced through, ran steady from his wrists; he went up some more; suddenly he no longer had the heart for it, he let himself fall under a tree.

The wind, stronger still, came through in great avalanches, with birds diverted like leaves, the trees bowing to the ground, and the flogged showers seemed to rise from below, cracking all around him. A purple lightning bolt tore through the middle of the sky, and remained there a long moment, fixed, like a vein in marble. He sat with his head in his hands, all of a sudden he stood up, he said: "Where is he? Ah! my God!", he fell back down.

When he came home in the evening, the storm raged on. He prayed all night. At least that's what recounted Benoît, Sophie's cousin, who had gone out around midnight, his cow ready to give birth; and so he recounted that, passing in front of Jean–Luc's, he had seen light, had heard a voice; that, returning three hours later, again he had seen light, had heard the voice once more; and that, not able to hold back, had climbed atop a heap of wood.

And, near the window, there was a table covered in cloth, beautiful and white; on the table, the crucifix with a little vase, some paper flowers, and a picture of the Sacré-Cœur; arranged farther ahead, a little dress, a bonnet, some stockings, some shoes; lastly, two shells, set there to look pretty. "It was like an altar," said the cousin. And, kneeling before it was Jean–Luc, who indeed prayed, his hands clasped together. "He looked like he was coming out of water," continued the cousin. And, wanting to come down from his heap of wood, a log had rolled out from under him, yet Jean–Luc had not heard a thing.

"You could've shot the cannon, he wouldn't have paid any attention."

The new tale spread from house to house, along with the tale from the previous evening; while the roofs dried, the roofs smoked a vapor, and the blue sky descended from between the fragments of the last clouds, the bad weather having gone to the Germans. Some little girls with very long skirts dragged a ram by its horns.

He tried everything. So, that same day, hoe in hand, he went off to the cemetery, and remained there until four o'clock; then they saw him enter Jéromette's house, from which he exited with a full basket of flower seedlings and a big watering can; went back to his task, which he continued until evening, coming to fill up his water can at the fountain from time to time. And those who out of curiosity had gone to the cemetery, did not recognize little Henri's tomb; up to that point it had remained exactly how it was the day of the funeral, the clods thrown in heaps, and bare, with nothing but the little cross, which was still planted crooked: the cross had now been straightened, the earth plowed, raked, watered, and all sorts of flowers had been planted, the pretty ones of summer: mignonette, china asters, marigolds, sweet peas. And so, because nearby, due to the great heat, the irises had wilted and the greenery had withered, the little tomb was the most beautiful, black in the middle of the gray and cracked earth. It even had a border made of flat stones, like the ones people cover roofs with, all of the same size and planted upright. Jéromette said: "He came and asked me, I gave him everything I had, after all it was for a tomb; and if I have to I'll go and water them myself, so that the poor things don't go thirsty."

But she did not need to; Jean-Luc watered them himself. The Sunday that followed, he went to Mass with devotion and left before everyone; then, instead of going to the square, he returned to the cemetery, he went to the tomb and began to pray on it. And, as they exited, the women who had remained for the vespers (which, in these parts, are said directly after Mass) watched the poor man in the distance, and took pity on him, thinking of his great suffering. While the men, on the contrary, because they have a harder heart, said: "Who knows how this will end!" And they repeated to Christine: "Be careful." But Jean-Luc seemed to have forgotten her.

He now moved as if swept by a great wind, no rest, no tranquility; he no longer said hello to anyone, his eyes turned to interior things, his ears occupied by a voice above him.

He no longer went to see anyone but the cobbler. The little pot of pitch was on the workbench, along with the thread and the awl; Nanche didn't cease his work, he continued to pull on his thread. He asked:

—You still haven't found him?

Jean-Luc shook his head. And Nanche:

—I understand you, I do.

He spoke with difficulty, his mouth full of the

wooden dowels he grabbed one after the other, and hammered with a firm stroke of the tool with the rounded end; for he was a good worker when he hadn't had anything to drink; and Jean-Luc leaned toward him:

—I showed goodwill for the property; I dug myself deep, but I resurfaced, I resurfaced purified . . .

He repeated: "Purified! . . . and I raised these things far from my mind; why is it they fall back upon me? . . ."

You could hear the little sound of the hammer against the leather, and far off in the village, accompanying it, the hammering of a scythe being sharpened for the second crops. Yet, that day, Nanche, planting his last dowel, and remaining with his hammer in the air:

—Do you want me to tell you? I know, I know where the little one is.

He raised a hand:

—Up there.

Jean-Luc answered:

—He would have waited for me.

The outline of roofs trembled against the sky, and everything seemed to fly in fragments through the air, because of the hot sun that dissolves and inhales.

He added:

—I did everything, and it was no use.

He sighed. He straightened his tall body, which folded itself back up, slumped, having lost more weight, which was visible because of his clothes, which had become too large, and were now in tatters. And the cobbler said again:

—We're miserable men.

But Jean-Luc was already off in the distance. His need for movement having grabbed hold of him again, he went straight ahead of himself; children would run away when they saw him now; someone watched from a window. A trail creeps under the cemetery and descends through the meadows toward La Zaut; he allowed himself to drift that way. He cut a baton from the hedge, trimmed it, skinned it, threw it: then took up his great strides again, with the stray appearance that was now his, halting suddenly, shaking his head.

Above him there was the great dry stone wall behind which they place the dead, who are happy, never having had the chance to sleep and rest as they pleased during their stay on Earth, and now departed below; seen thus from the ground, the steeple points in the air without the rest of the church, the very tip is cut off.

All of a sudden, standing there, Jean-Luc saw something move in the meadows. It was a woman with a very small child, whom she held in her lap. She was sitting at the foot of the hedge, she undid her camisole, then pressing the child against her, she began to breastfeed him. He approached, recognized Christine.

And felt jealous.

CHAPTER XI

JEALOUS OF THIS CHILD OF HERS, when he no longer had his own. He spied on her from inside a bush. She was there, so close, she who turned her back to him as she bent over, the nape of her neck showed, bronzed underneath the black bun, with its little copper combs. And, holding the child under the head, she clasped him to her chest; she said: "Drink little one, drink my boy." Then moved him to the other side. And Jean-Luc thought: "She's got one, my God!" Still thinking back to what she had said the day he had driven her out: "You've got yours, I've got mine."

But the little one was satisfied; she buttoned her blouse; following which, rising, she took the child on her arm, took the rake lying near her—and went off, climbing back up the path. And Jean-Luc followed her, sneaking behind the hedges.

But suddenly he hid inside a bush again, having seen the daughter of the bell ringer arrive, who was on her way down, and bumped into Christine—who stopped, and the two of them began to chat. He listened. Ludivine said:

—How's the little one?

Christine responded:

—He's well, thanks.

She showed him to her. He could see the little bonnet, the big cheeks, just like Henri's were in the past, in the cradle—and the two women bent over him: "He's so beautiful, how old is he?" "Three months old." "Only three months, and so big, and so strong! What do you give him?"

Christine was standing upright, her rake against her shoulder, she beat on her chest:

—I've got plenty here.

Jean-Luc lost his breath; he was crouching, leaning on his hands, he felt them shake under him.

—That's right, continued Christine, as long as he wants it, I've got some right here.

Ludivine continued:

—You're not like Josette, she had to put hers under the goat.

They laughed upright in the sunshine.

—You see, said Christine, mine eats when he's hungry, he sleeps well, he doesn't cry, he's a sweet boy.

And when Christine had gone off, Ludivine cried to her again from afar:

—When will you be done with the second crop?

—Almost done, two more days in these parts, and then I'll only have Tové left.

Once again, he followed her, and up at the top of the

path, the tip of the village appears, made up of wheat barns and haylofts, high on their pillars of stone, which is where he went to hide, making a detour to watch her pass.

He didn't resurface the entire day, except around sunset when he came to pray under the Cerniou cross, for, since the Sunday they had found him kneeling in the cemetery, he had prayed before all the crosses.

He remained under the Cerniou cross until nighttime, he came home; the little empty cradle was there; he carried it to the kitchen, and, grabbing an ax, chopped it to pieces. He walked over to the little garments, the dress, the stockings, and the bonnet, which he used to make a little package he tied with a string, and placed into a chest, which he locked, holding on to the key.

And at length he remained collapsed on a chair; then, all of a sudden, stood up, returned to the kitchen, and, leaning over the fragments of the cradle, he grabbed them one by one, trying to put them back together, he thought: "If only he would return!" And he felt regret; so he went back to the chest, took out the package, undid it, put away the clothes like before.

He sat back down, pondered things. He got back up, pondered things. He made an effort. He came and went in great strides through the bedroom; in the stillness of night, the whole house trembled and cracked. For a while, the sound of footsteps continued, with the lamp on, and the square of light that dimly marked the meadow; he told himself: "I have to keep trying," and looked out the windows to see whether the sky grew pale, for the night had advanced, not much however, but he no longer had any perception of the time you measure with accuracy in your everyday life, until one day you're ejected from it.

So much so that it was not quite daybreak when Augustin, who had woken very early to scythe, and had just entered the barn, heard someone call to him. He was about to come out with his scythe; he didn't recognize the voice. He peeped through a crack between the beams, saw Jean-Luc. But quite another man, with his pallor, with his shirt open underneath his unbuttoned vest, his head bare, and his long hair falling on his forehead; so that Augustin took fright, and didn't answer, went to hide in the corner behind the door, while this man called for him once again.

It was that pleasant hour when the houses wake, along with the kitchen lamps; all over the paths there are men on their way; the herd of goats has already gone, guided by the little shepherd, and there's a fire on the tip of the mountains. But Jean-Luc called a third time. And Augustin, because he was beginning to feel ashamed, and thinking that Jean-Luc would enter if he didn't come out, appeared all of a sudden, his scythe in hand.

—What do you want?

Jean-Luc had come forward—and as Augustin moved away, on his guard:

—Don't be afraid, he began to say. I just want to speak with you.

He repeated:

—I want to speak with you.

Augustin answered: "Alright, I'm listening." Jean-Luc lowered his voice and with haste: "Go to Christine and advise her to leave! straightaway, today or tomorrow, you understand."

Augustin said to him:

—I will, but I need to know why.

—You see, it's the little one. She's the reason he went away. So here's what I've been thinking: if she goes, he'll return; but, you see, I just can't, I can't go on living without him.

—And what will she think if I tell her: "Be off"? Does she not have a right to be in the village like you do, owning a house like you do?

—You will tell her you're coming on my behalf. Otherwise . . . tragedy!

Jean-Luc was shaking, was it because of the cool air or did he have a fever? His hands were as restless as leaves in the wind, his entire body too, and his large shoulders, however accustomed to the great weight of hay loads, were all too weak under this other weight—then he pointed to the clouds in the air:

—They're headed in the right direction.

He inhaled the air:

—The air is cool, it no longer gives me any pleasure.

With that, something else in him broke, he continued:

—You see, I've come because I've forgotten it all,

and perhaps she'll listen to you because she loves you, and you can be with her now, it no longer matters to me; she's no longer the one that I need.

He grabbed a fallen leaf:

—This right here, this is her.

So Augustin said to him:

—Why don't you go and see her yourself?

He placed a hand on his heart:

—It would cause me too much pain, I've got an open wound right here.

—Well then! I'll go! said Augustin.

But he did not keep his promise. Where he did go, was to the village and to the inn, and repeated it all, even inflating the truth. He finished by saying: "He should be locked up." But Jean-Luc was not locked up, and three more days passed. In the end he made up his mind.

He made one last effort, he went to her himself. This section of the village is on a slope; there are, between the houses, narrow little passages, which one descends through and sinks deep inside of; and above, the roofs touch each other, so that you can barely see the sky. Christine lived there; the house had two stories and her bedroom was located on the second floor. Jean-Luc went up the stairs, he knocked at the door, Félicie was singing, she stopped singing; then the little one started to cry, and a voice said: "Is that you, Augustin?" He answered: "No, it's not Augustin, it's me." Once again they didn't recognize his voice.

Then, Jean-Luc pushed the door open, and at once she saw him, he who was standing at the threshold, without entering. Because the entranceway was so small, he was forced to lower his head; and yet he looked so tall and fearsome, less because of his height than because of his appearance, with his pallor and sad eyes, so tall and fearsome to her, who remained speechless as she watched him. The little one was on the table, for she had been swaddling him; but, standing there, she hid him; he didn't see him at first. What he did see, was the kitchen and poor Félicie, who opened her mouth, and a sort of scream escaped. The fire was blazing, daylight filtered in through the window, some dust danced through the sunlight. He said:

—I've come.

But, as soon as he took one step inside, she cried:

—This is not your home.

He halted, he said:

—I'm well aware this is not my home, but I want the truth to be out; there are two of us, that's one too many.

She answered him:

—You're not worth listening to.

—One too many! he said, you have to go.

And he looked her in the face. But, just then, she picked up the child, whom he saw all of a sudden, and he looked away. Then, without looking up:

—It's my advice to you: be off while you can.

She didn't seem worried about him, and Jean-Luc, still looking down:

—To avoid a tragedy.

He continued: "Do you understand?" He said: "A tragedy! a tragedy! because I did everything and you did nothing; will you answer me?" She answered: "Leave me alone."

He closed the door, he ran down the stairs.

A while later, Marie, who was hanging up her washing on the garden wall, called her husband: "Come quickly!" He was busy shoeing a mule brought over by a girl who was standing near the beast; he dropped his pliers and came. Marie said to him: "Look over there."

Jean-Luc was once again under the cross, no longer kneeling, but bowed all the way down to the earth, and the great cross with its golden Christ rose above him. And, behind the cross, the painter's house, all flowering with geraniums, emerged with honey-colored wood; then, in the sky, like boats beneath their sails, the clouds, filled with wind, glided by calmly—Jean-Luc was before the cross and was flat on his face.

At once he straightened himself; he looked up toward the Christ and his arms were wide open.

—My God! what's the matter with him? said Marie.

And the girl with the mule was also there watching, with the worker, with some neighbors: his arms wide open, his body thrown back; then, as if under a weight that slowly reappeared, he fell forward once more; he pleaded again, fell back again; and the Christ hung from the wood, his hands, his feet pierced by nails, with his thin hollow body, a wound at his side, his crown of thorns; and Jean-Luc was screaming: "Let me go!" Then he took the bottom of the cross in his arms as if to beg for mercy, but it was most likely refused to him, for he continued aloud: "Must I? Is it possible?" And a passing woman heard him.

He prayed some more, he prayed; then at once he rose and returned with great strides, nodding his head; he was saying: "I must! I must!"

CHAPTER XII

NOON HAD JUST SOUNDED, Jean-Luc took some matches, two or three pieces of thick wood, a bit of rope; hid all of it in his shirt, near his leather belt; came out, locked the door, and went off in the direction of Tové.

It was the tenth of September; the sky remained clear, despite a few clouds resembling those in the morning, and a fine autumn mist hung somewhere in the heights of the sky, but the drought had caused a few trees to yellow, and on the bank slopes the grass was dry and brittle. He walked quickly, and, having left the village, went straight down to the fields below the church. Someone who worked in those parts cried to him: "Where are you going, Jean-Luc?" He didn't turn around, on the contrary he hastened his walk, the other man thought: "His madness has got a hold of him."

He was soon in the woods. A little ways down there's a field that cuts through it; this is the place they call Tové. As he approached it, Jean-Luc slowed his pace, and he walked with precaution among the dead branches; you couldn't hear a thing, not a crack; he went from tree to tree, grabbing on to the trunks, hiding behind them, and arrived to the field in this manner.

Christine was there. Of the second crop, she only had two squares left to dry, which she had scythed the previous night and the night before that; gray among the short lawn, she flipped them over, handling the rake, thrusting it forward, her hands slipped along the handle, and she lifted her arms in the daylight. The sun, already a little lower in the sky, illuminated her along with that part of the field, while the shadows of the woods fell at the other end; that's where she had put the child down, having formed a little bed of dry grass for him, and placed a rolled up cloth under his head and a handkerchief over his face, because of the flies and the grasshoppers. The little one slept, he didn't stir; as for her, she hurried, alone as she was.

Jean-Luc didn't move either. From his hiding place, you could glimpse the back of the valley, as if veiled in muslin, pierced by the tips of rocks here and there; and then the slope came, rising toward him, and covered in fields and in woods—there was no one around, except for over there on the path, very far, from time to time, a man passing by; then a girl who sat on a mule that had a big stomach and skinny legs; she too disappeared.

Meanwhile, Christine, who was done flipping over the second square, went to the first one, saw it was dry, went to get a floor cloth, which she brought over and stretched out, piling the dry grass on top of it, then folded up the four corners and tied them together; it formed something like a great ball, which she took with her, bowing under it; beneath her camisole, you could see her strong waist extending and flexing.

She made a second, a third trip, coming back up the field, all red and sweating; from time to time, she went to see what the child was doing, and lifted the handkerchief, but he slept soundly; she returned straightaway, going off with a load again; and so, by the sixth time, the first square was brought in.

Following which, she went to see if the second square had sufficiently dried; she picked up a handful of hay that she crumpled between her fingers; undoubtedly it hadn't fully dried, and she would have to wait, for once again she went to the child, took him in her arms and returned to the hayloft.

The sun was strong, she still had one or two hours left to work; it's best to wait in the shade—and the wind had picked up, so that she returned; and Jean-Luc, watching her, saw her turn the corner of the hayloft. It was a very small hayloft, old, leaning to one side, made of blackened beams, with a large overhanging roof; it had in fact been repaired in the spring, and the remaining beams and planks were nearby. It was already nearly full, at least in the back, as was made visible by the wisps and clumps of hay that jutted out through the cracks; the largest pile was in the back, the second crop's smallest heap was up front; and Jean-Luc knew this; yet he remained where he was for some time.

Nothing stirred anymore except for the hot air trembling over the field. It was completely deserted; little birds were letting themselves fall from the tops of trees into the grass (they barely opened their wings), and pricked where they fell with their beaks, sometimes turning their heads to the side: yellow butterflies fluttered languidly on the short lawn, seeking a flower they could no longer find, or took shelter in the swath; and the shadows of the woods had expanded little by little, expanding more and more toward the second square, which still needed to dry.

All of a sudden Jean-Luc rose.

He swiftly crossed the field to the back of the hayloft; he let himself fall to a crouch.

He listened: everything kept quiet.

Nothing but the susurrus of grasshoppers in the hay; he heard his watch tick too; he placed his hand over it as if to muffle the sound.

A crow cried over the woods—he thrust himself forward, he began to crawl to the door, and, gluing his face to the beams, watched through a little hole.

Christine was right near him, outstretched in the hay: she had nodded off; the child, who had slid from her arms, slept sideways on her skirts. Her head was slightly drooping and her upper body was leaning to one side, she napped quietly, with one hand under the nape of her neck, and dreams behind her forehead. Pretty to behold in this way, with her thin blue eyelids, lowered and taut over her big beautiful eyes, and the movement under her camisole, while her other hand hung limp by her strong leg, which was exposed up to the calf under the big blue cotton stocking.

Jean-Luc took the rope out of his pocket.

The door of the hayloft was of wood, with an iron ring; there was another ring on the mount, for a chain to slide through.

In one swift movement, Jean-Luc rushed forward, pushed the door, slid the rope through the ring, tied a first knot, a second, and she, woken with a jolt, did not even have the time to cry out: "Who's there?" before Jean-Luc had already moved back, taken the matches out of his pocket. And she, thinking it was a joke:

—Let me get up first! This is no way to approach a sleeping woman.

He looked to see whether the hayloft was down-wind, yes, the wind came from the right direction; he had calmly started to arrange the wood. All of a sudden, a great scream sounded, Christine had seen him. She cried: "Jean-Luc! Jean-Luc!" And threw herself against the door, which she shook with both hands, having grabbed it by the crosstie; but her fingers kept sliding off, and the rope was sturdy; at that moment she no longer had the heart to go on, she said:

—Jean-Luc, what are you doing?

He didn't answer. He struck a match, the strong wind extinguished it; he struck a second one, and, while

143

the sulfur took fire, he kneeled upright, and shielded the match with both hands.

She understood.

—Jesus! Jesus! she cried, is this even possible?

And then:

—Jean-Luc, forgive me, I was wrong, I know that now, I won't do it again. My big friend, my man, you'll come home, we'll kiss . . .

She went on, thinking of Augustin:

—Do what you will with him, I'll help you if I have to, I'll bring him to you, say, is that what you want? It's true, I was with him, but I don't love him anymore, you're the one I love!

He didn't listen. The fire started with difficulty; it seemed as if hours went by.

She opened her mouth, a scream came out again, hoarse and prolonged; then words returned to her: "Help! Help!" But nothing. In response, the wind in the trees, the cry of the crickets; nobody in the fields, nobody on the path either. Down in the valley, a train passed by once more; life goes on in this way. And so, seized by fury:

—Bandit! she cried.

Then she started to beg again: "Jean-Luc, please, because I've always thought: he has a good heart, let me go and I will thank you." And, anger taking hold of her again, she threw herself at the door, running along the wall that she scratched and flayed with her nails, her hair fallen over her eyes, her camisole entirely ripped, her bare

144

arm showing among the tatters of fabric, and the little one shrieked, having rolled away from her in the hay.

She grabbed him, she held him out to Jean-Luc.

—Take him at least, she said, he hasn't done anything wrong; he's an innocent! yes, you can keep me, but let him go. Look at his pretty hair and his little mouth, no teeth yet, that such a small child should die!

She started to weep, she kissed the child among her tears. Jean-Luc was not listening. The fire was rising; Christine rolled on the floor, she was writhing in pain. The flame had already grown; the wind fanned it now, it shot to the roof, it cracked, curving at the tip. Then, with another gust of wind, the blaze reddened from underneath, and suddenly regained in size. A white smoke rose, soon folding down, running across the roof, then spreading out; it turned blue and thinned out, the flame touched the edge of the roof; the twigs jutting out took fire one after the other. And Jean-Luc was happy and began to smile.

The screams diminished, now muted, as if exhausted; the screams ceased. For, having moved back and rolled into the hay, she no longer struggled now—knees up, hiding the child in the hollow of her skirt, she watched death come with wide eyes, and waited.

A burnt beam collapsed under the weight of the roof, and the wind dug into the bare haystack, forming a sort of red cave; again he examined his work, saw it was good, then went off running. And, once at the edge of the woods, he turned around: the fire continued to spread, erect like a column above the hayloft; the smell of smoke traveled far; he went off toward Le Bourni; he had already bypassed it, through the tunnel of the bisse, when the smoke bell started to ring.

CHAPTER XIII

A SCREAM SOUNDED IN THE VILLAGE, a race for help, but it was on foot; when they arrived, nothing was left of the hayloft; what did remain was the haystack, bare and blackening; they planted great metal hooks inside of it and they mowed it down.

And sometime before sunset, the four chosen men had already left, climbing up toward the mayens where they had seen Jean-Luc go off. There was his cousin Théodule, and old Romain, who were both in Sassette, the counselor Chrétien Rey, and a plainclothes officer.

They walked with haste. First the land is flat, you pass the sawmill, the wheel was stopped; the sawyer cried: "I saw him too, he went up through the meadows over there." The officer said: "We're going in the right direction." Next you enter the woods; the birds were going to bed; the path turning narrow, the men walked behind one another. You go up, they went up; and all of a sudden, in the forest, you arrive at one of the ponds, calm and beautiful water, the canal on one side, and the whole way around, trees that had grown inside of it; you walk alongside the pond, and these parts resemble a park, with squares of grass, a fine grass like the one on lawns, and beautiful bouquets of larches that seemed arranged all around, as well as streams that flow through the moss; then a smooth trail, without stones, that looks covered in sand—which they continued to follow all the way to the second berm above. These vast plateaus are covered with thin grass, which advances like waves that move from one side to another, before dying afar between knolls. There the four men were caught in the fog.

And the night was on its way too; they saw it would be impossible to go any farther that evening, and went to sleep in a hayloft; they made a fire before the door, they sat around it. The flames lit the sky suspiciously, in the same way they flicker upon a ceiling, then quickly diminished; they pulled some bread and cheese from a bag they had brought, along with a bottle of eau-de-vie; they ate and drank.

Next, they went to sleep, lying down on the hay. Little by little the flames dimmed and the fog fell upon them like a lid smothering embers; the last cinders were already emitting black smoke. But the clouds still descended little by little, as sometimes happens when they form around the mountain peaks in the evening, and crept slowly all the way to the back of the valley. In the morning, the sky was immaculate. It turned white toward the Orient; and this first light, like a sheaf one releases, opened up at the base of the sky; then the brightness increased with, above, a flame shining on the tips of boulders; and the birds cried out in the great calm of the morning.

They were already up; they immediately set off. The trail crosses the forest once more, only it's narrower, rockier, hollowed out by the rain, it veers, then climbs straight up: the fir trees dwindle, replaced by the larches and their light greenery; at once, on a new berm, where you can still scythe, the mayens appear, seven or eight of them, forming a very small village. Sometimes you can find a kitchen or a room there; a window will be shining under the shadow of a roof.

The officer said: "Watch out!"; the four men walked a little farther through the woods. Then, at the border, they dispersed, but not high enough, they couldn't see anything; which is why Théodule walked a little bit farther to the side, climbing up a bank; and once higher up, suddenly waved to the others, who came. And so it was that, from where they stood, they discovered Jean-Luc's mayen, small and a little closer than the others, with Jean-Luc in front of it.

They saw him clearly, they recognized him without hesitation due to his beard and his untidy shirt, but they thought: "What is he doing?" There he was, sitting in front of the door, not on the steps, but on the ground; and at times he looked up, and laughed, as if he were talking to someone, at times he kept his head down as if he were busy with a task. He had made little piles of dirt, all tidy in a row; he had planted green branches and flowers in these little piles; all around, with fir tree needles, he had built a sort of fence: it was a little garden. They understood; they thought: "He thinks he's found the little one."

And they noticed, too, how happy Jean-Luc now seemed, for he smiled the entire time, or laughed, his mouth open; and went on with his task, now beginning to build a second garden. Then, standing up, he went to a nearby spring, filled the inside of his hat with water and emptied it in a little channel dug for this purpose; and it became a stream, and underneath, there was a dyke with a wisp of straw: it formed a fountain.

—You see, they said to each other, it's taken hold of him again.

And one of them:

—That's why he started the fire.

And the other men:

—You think?

—Yes of course, to get him back. And he's happy about the fire, because he has him back now.

And so they asked themselves:

—What should we do?

They went back to where they'd been standing. Then, coming out all together, they approached the mayen. Théodule cried:

—Give yourself up, Jean-Luc!

But he, having seen them, suddenly stood up, he answered:

—He's mine, you won't take him from me.

And escaped, clutching the child, clutching the void in his arms, running uphill with all of his strength, on the slope, where the others chased him; but he ran with a strength beyond the strength of an ordinary man; so that they quickly gave up, and having regrouped once more, held council. For they were drawn into the chase and thrilled by this latest escape, which they now discussed, one of them saying:

—He'll get away if he gets to Les Roffes.

Another one:

—If we aren't the ones to grab him, there will always be someone to stop him over there.

Théodule:

—I think he's gone to the chalet.

Upon which, they decided to go to the chalet and have a look. There is another steep hill, another forest to cross, where the first boulders appear; and there on top, like a wall, the pastures begin to show. And even farther, the grass ceases at once, and the rockery begins, upon which the last ridges rise, with their great precipitous walls, with no further trails, or else impassable, except in one or two places, where there are cols with marked passages. So, toward the Orient, the pastures unfurl in the distance; toward the Occident, on the contrary, they're abruptly cut off by a deep notch, which is the top of the gorges of La Zaut. There, a saber has slashed into the mountain; it falls apart stone by stone and crumbles through the wood passages, molded by the frost, with, above, what look like leaning towers, mined by the foot, along with some cracked rocky grounds. But the snow lasts in the folds, which explains why the gray stone was stained white in certain places.

Through the last larches and the mountain pines that surfaced, they urged each other on once more. The sun was strong, for the shade had made itself sparse, large tree-less areas and only a few miserable branches left to those that remained. The great buzzing of flies sounded, and from over there, toward La Zaut, there rose, similar to a great wind, the roar of water, which you could see hanging from a knoll a little higher up, in waterfalls, forming a bend and awakening. The nails on their shoes screeched as they gnawed into the stone; because they had picked up their pace, the four men did not speak anymore. They passed near a great larch that had been struck down by lightning, with no remaining branches, with nothing but its big blackened trunk, hollow in the middle; and all around it the thin ground was dressed in clumps of juniper, with here and there, on the banks of stone that pierced through, blocks of compost glued together; and soon even the mountain pines were smaller, now stunted and rocky; then there's a tiny path, carved into the rock, with a cow fence running alongside the void, and, from there, you arrive at the pasture.

It spreads across rather flat large spaces; and in some areas of the short and grazed grass, the tall gentians appeared, with their thick and glistening leaves.

The chalet is farther up; the chalet was empty, because the herd had left two or three days earlier.

You saw it in the distance, short beneath its roof, coarse with its dry stone walls, a door in front, but no window or chimney, and nearby, in a hollow, there was a great pond of green water, with muddy banks, pierced with holes by the hooves of cows. Nothing stirred. And everything looked small, due to the great wall that rises behind the chalet and seems to lean forward, because of how steep it is; the chalet was small, smaller still were the four men, who had halted, not having found anything.

They hesitated a moment, then sat down at the edge of the stream and started eating again, for running provokes hunger, and the fresh air digs a hole in your stomach. And they didn't suspect they had been found, it was the truth, however: Jean-Luc was hidden, a little higher up than the chalet, behind the great quarter of a boulder; he had chosen this spot because of the moss, upon which he had put down the child, or so he thought. And from there he spied on the men.

They were still talking, you could hear their voices, but could not understand what they were saying. Jean-Luc watched their gestures, one of them pointing to the rocks, the other to the pastures; time passed; the sun calmly rose in the sky, supported on each side by the columns of the mountains.

And you saw Théodule flip the bottle, showing them it was empty, so they pulled another one out of the bag, and the glass again passed from hand to hand, the four men in a circle; and far below them the great land opened up, with all of its rich plains, from which a lukewarm air rose, and the echoes of the sounds of men.

Then they closed the bag back up, and ascended toward the chalet: the door was shut, but not locked, for there's no lock, and no one leaves anything inside it: as they approached, they slowed their pace, walking with precaution, and Jean-Luc heard Théodule saying: "He might be inside." And so two of them entered, while the other two remained at the door; the two who had entered probably searched the chalet's nooks and crannies, for they stayed inside a long time, but finally came out again, shaking their heads; then Romain stomped his foot and said: "Hell!" For he was peeved, and the others too; at the time they were losing. And one of them repeated: "He went off toward Les Roffes." And the others: "What would he do there?" "If it was up to me," said Théodule, "I'd go and have another look in the sheep enclosure, and then never mind, go back down."

And as they were beginning to climb through the rocks that had rolled down, all of a sudden, they heard a great cry, which rooted them to the spot, and Jean-Luc, lifting his empty arms in the air, came out from where he was hiding, and cried once again: "You won't have him!" Then he left again, extending his long legs, leaning forward in the haste of his escape; upon which the others, motionless for an instant, hurled themselves behind him, while the counselor cried: "We've got him!" And the officer said while running: "Two of us should make a right to cut him off, in case he heads in the other direction." So the counselor and Romain took off on the right, making a detour, while Jean-Luc continued to climb straight ahead, the two other men following him closely, for now he was visible from a distance on the more open terrain, even though he was in the lead; and at times he ran without turning around, at times he turned around, setting off again with new momentum.

Théodule cried a second time: "Give yourself up Jean-Luc, what can you do against the four of us?" He formed a bullhorn with his hands: "Give yourself up," he said, "we won't hurt you." The echo returned his words, but Jean-Luc didn't stop. "Let him be, we'll get a hold of him at the boulders." And indeed, off to the right, the two men pulled away then spaced out, and Théodule and the officer spaced out too, in case Jean-Luc came back down; but no sound could be heard passing over the fine lawn, where the soles of shoes get caught. At times they looked up, and there, a hundred meters from them, Jean-Luc passed by a sheep enclosure on a little eminence, walked to the back of it, where they followed him, then he reappeared, opposite the cliff face.

One more movement, and there he was. Then the shadow of a cloud came, enveloping him, and from the tips of the boulders, it fell upon him in what looked like an unfolded fabric; they saw him turn around, then he stood his back against the boulders. And so the officer shouted: "Watch out!", and began to run, along with the other three men. But Jean-Luc burst into laughter.

He was standing there, arms over the load he still thought that he carried, and was leaning over it, considering it with fire and love; the wind ruffled his beard, he had lost his hat. He looked up and said softly (for the others were close enough to hear): "Come, but you'll never have him."

And there was no space left to him but the space toward the gorge; it opened up over there, cut distinctly from the edge; a fence ran along it, made of intertwined shards of wood; he looked that way and continued: "The Good Lord has returned him to me, I'll return him to the Good Lord . . ." At that moment, the sun reappeared and the smooth rock glistened in the great radiant daylight. He leaned over the child, he kissed him twice. Next he said: "It's over," and he said: "You'll say adieu for me and pray for him and me." And he hurled himself toward the gorge.

—Run! cried the officer to Théodule, run, cut him off!

The other two, having arrived, followed him with difficulty, and the officer too, overtaken on the left; while Théodule ran right to the top with all of his strength, but it was too late; and all of a sudden they no longer had the heart for it, they all looked away—only the officer watched. He cried again:

—What are you doing? My God! What are you doing?

And then: "Grab him!", for Jean-Luc had arrived at the fence, had jumped over it, and, standing at the ledge overlooking the void, had turned around one last time, to say:

—Come now!

And so they saw him kneel and begin to pray, upon which the officer, still hoping to reach him, hurled himself toward him, but Jean-Luc was already standing again; he slowly lifted his arms in the air as if they held a substantial weight, which he then threw before him into the void; he leaned forward, as if to watch it fall; and then it was his turn, he moved back, he gained momentum.

They had remained where they were standing, pale and breathless. Théodule said: "Damned!" Romain repeated: "Damned!" Everything was calm, a second cloud passed; the sound of water hadn't changed, mingled with the long murmur of the wind; the light dimmed once more, then reappeared, casting shadows aside.

They allowed time to pass, no longer sure of anything. Then Théodule said: "We have to go." And three of them descended into the gorge while the fourth ran to the village. They found Jean-Luc on a stone bank.

The torrent's water was passing just near him, sliding

soundlessly in its smooth bed; the men lifted the body; it was hard work, it took some time.

They had wrapped a cloth around his head; they said: "It cracked like a nut; the brains leapt out."

There were open doors, lanterns, voices; Jean-Luc was heavy to carry all the way to his bed, where he remained lifeless.

And he was tall on the bed; he was ever so tall.

CHARLES-FERDINAND RAMUZ (born Sept. 24, 1878, Cully, Switzerland—died May 23, 1947, Pully, near Lausanne) was a Swiss novelist whose realistic, poetic, and somewhat allegorical stories of man against nature made him one of the most iconic French-Swiss writers of the twentieth century. As a young man, he moved to Paris to pursue a life of writing, where he struck up a friendship with Igor Stravinsky, later writing the libretto for *The Soldier's Tale* (1918). Returning to Switzerland in 1914, he spent the rest of his life living and writing in the canton of Vaud, where he was born. Ramuz pioneered a common Swiss literary identity, writing books about mountaineers, farmers, or villagers engaging in often tragic struggles against catastrophe. His legacy is remembered through the Ramuz Foundation, which grants the quintannual literary award, the Grand Prix C.F. Ramuz, for Swiss writers in the French language, and his portrait is featured on the 200 Swiss franc note.

OLIVIA BAES is a Franco-American multidisciplinary artist who grew up between France, Catalonia, and the United States. She holds a Bachelor's Degree in Comparative Literature and a Master of the Arts in Cultural Translation from the American University of Paris. She has written multiple feature-length screenplays, including *L'Homme au piano* and *Riches,* which was selected as a project in development for the 70th Cannes Film Festival. Her translations include a co-translation of *Me & Other Writing* by Marguerite Duras (Dorothy, a Publishing Project, 2019).

Thank you all
for your support.
We do this for you,
and could not do
it without you.

 DEEP
VELLUM

PARTNERS

FORTHCOMING FROM DEEP VELLUM

AMANG · *Raised by Wolves*
translated by Steve Bradbury · TAIWAN

MARIO BELLATIN · *Mrs. Murakami's Garden*
translated by Heather Cleary · MEXICO

MAGDA CARNECI · *FEM*
translated by Sean Cotter · ROMANIA

MIRCEA CĂRTĂRESCU · *Solenoid*
translated by Sean Cotter · ROMANIA

MATHILDE CLARK · *Lone Star*
translated by Martin Aitken · DENMARK

LOGEN CURE · *Welcome to Midland: Poems* · USA

PETER DIMOCK · *Daybook from Sheep Meadow* · USA

CLAUDIA ULLOA DONOSO · *Little Bird*, translated by Lily Meyer · PERU/NORWAY

LEYLÂ ERBIL · *A Strange Woman*
translated by Nermin Menemencioğlu · TURKEY

ROSS FARRAR · *Ross Sings Cheree & the Animated Dark: Poems* · USA

FERNANDA GARCIA LAU · *Out of the Cage*
translated by Will Vanderhyden · ARGENTINA

ANNE GARRÉTA · *In/concrete*
translated by Emma Ramadan · FRANCE

GOETHE · *Faust*
translated by Zsuzsanna Ozsváth and Frederick Turner · GERMANY

PERGENTINO JOSÉ · *Red Ants: Stories*
translated by Tom Bunstead and the author · MEXICO

JUNG YOUNG MOON · *Arriving in a Thick Fog*
translated by Mah Eunji and Jeffrey Karvonen · SOUTH KOREA

TAISIA KITAISKAIA · *The Nightgown & Other Poems* · USA

DMITRY LIPSKEROV · *The Tool and the Butterflies*
translated by Reilly Costigan-Humes & Isaac Stackhouse Wheeler · RUSSIA

FISTON MWANZA MUJILA · *The Villain's Dance*, translated by Roland Glasser · *The River in the Belly: Selected Poems*, translated by Bret Maney · DEMOCRATIC REPUBLIC OF CONGO

GORAN PETROVIĆ · *At the Lucky Hand, aka The Sixty-Nine Drawers*
translated by Peter Agnone · SERBIA

LUDMILLA PETRUSHEVSKAYA · *Kidnapped: A History of Crimes*, translated by Marian Schwartz ·
The New Adventures of Helen: Magical Tales, translated by Jane Bugaeva · RUSSIA

JULIE POOLE · *Bright Specimen: Poems from the Texas Herbarium* · USA

MANON STEFAN ROS · *The Blue Book of Nebo* · WALES

ETHAN RUTHERFORD · *Farthest South & Other Stories* · USA

TATIANA RYCKMAN · *The Ancestry of Objects* · USA

MUSTAFA STITOU · *Two Half Faces*
translated by David Colmer · NETHERLANDS

BOB TRAMMELL · *The Origins of the Avant-Garde in Dallas & Other Stories* · USA